The Big Glass

GABRIEL JOSIPOVICI

The Big Glass

CARCANET

First published in 1991 by
Carcanet Press Limited
208-212 Corn Exchange Buildings
Manchester M4 3BQ

Quotations from the 'Protevangelium of James' come from
The Apocryphal New Testament, translated and edited by M.R. James
(Oxford, 1924). Pages 57-59 were published as 'The Death of Images'
in *PN Review* 13:2 (1986).

British Library Cataloguing in Publication Data

Josipovici, Gabriel, *1940-*
    The big glass.
    I. Title
    821.914

ISBN 0 85635 905 X

The publisher acknowledges the financial assistance
of the Arts Council of Great Britain.

Set in 10½pt Garamond by Bryan Williamson, Darwen
Printed and bound in England by SRP Ltd, Exeter

. . . those pleasures which bear no relation
to the gratifications we experience in
scratching ourselves.

Plato: *Philebus*

Note

This is not a fictionalized biography of Marcel Duchamp. Nevertheless, it could obviously not have been written without the existence of Duchamp's *Large Glass*, his notes to the glass known as the Green Box, and the scattering of other writings and interviews by him. Octavio Paz's *Marcel Duchamp or the Castle of Purity* has also been a source of inspiration.

To
Christopher Couch
Stephen Finer
&
Andrzej Jackowski

I began work on the big glass on 27 July 1967, wrote
Harsnet. Goldberg, images of their last meeting in the narrow entrance of the elegant little Scottish National Gallery
of Modern Art dancing in his head, slipped a sheet of A4
into his old Olivetti portable and started to transcribe. I
began work on the big glass on 27 July 1967, he typed. I
had been preparing myself for that moment for a long time,
he typed, as Harsnet had written. I had been preparing
myself for as long as I can remember, preparing myself
(though I did not always realize it) from the day that I was
born, preparing myself, wrote Harsnet (typed Goldberg),
but always aware of the dangers of beginning too soon. For
there is nothing worse, he wrote, than beginning too soon.
It is much worse to begin too soon, he wrote, than not to
begin at all. Much worse to begin too soon than to begin
too late. Much worse to begin too soon and realize one has
begun too soon than to begin too late and realize one has
begun too late. Much worse to begin too soon and realize
one is inadequately prepared than to begin too late and realize
one is over-prepared. Much worse to begin too soon and
reach the end too quickly, typed Goldberg, squinting at the
manuscript before him, than to begin at the right time and
reach the end too quickly. Much worse to begin too soon
and feel one has begun too soon than to begin at the right time
and discover one has nothing to begin. That is why, wrote
Harsnet, I have been preparing myself for that moment for
a long time, that is why I have cleared the decks and prepared
the ground, because unless the decks are cleared and the
ground prepared there is little hope of succeeding in what
one has planned to do, little hope of achieving anything of

9

lasting value, though lasting is a relative term and so is value and whatever it is one has planned to do is certain to be altered in the process, which does not of course mean, he wrote, that one can start anywhere at any time. It is just because whatever one has planned to do is bound to be altered in the process that it is important to start at the right moment, he wrote. It is *just because* whatever one has planned is bound to change as one proceeds that it is fatal to start too soon or too late, though it may be no less fatal, he wrote (and Goldberg typed), to start at the right time, for then there is no excuse, no excuse whatsoever. I have done with excuses, wrote Harsnet (typed Goldberg), I have done with excuses towards myself and towards others, that is the meaning of the right time, he wrote, that I have done with excuses, that I have used up all the excuses and reached the bottom of excuses, that I have wrung the neck of excuses, that I have settled the hash of excuses. To begin at the right time, he wrote, means to be done with excuses once and for all. *Excuses*, wrote Goldberg in the margin of his typescript with a felt-tip pen, *an end to excuses*. There has to be a time, wrote Harsnet, and Goldberg, laying down the pen, began to type again, there has to be a time when excuses are no longer necessary, will never again be necessary, there has to be such a time in everybody's life, when too soon and too late no longer mean anything, a time, wrote Harsnet (typed Goldberg), when one starts because one starts and for no other reason. But to arrive at that moment, he wrote, it is necessary to be patient, it is necessary to hold back, it is often necessary to do nothing. All my life, he wrote, I have been preparing myself for this moment, but if I have prepared myself correctly then it is so that when the moment came I should not be encumbered with the sensation of having waited for it all my life, for such a sensation, wrote Harsnet, is too heavy a burden for anyone to carry. The right moment to begin, he wrote, is the moment when right and wrong are no longer an issue, it may even be the moment, he wrote, when the realization dawns and is at once accepted that another moment might have been equally valid, and when this no longer matters. This is the moment and that is all. There is also the practical element to be considered, he wrote. There is the clearing of the room, the removal of any trace of what had previously filled it. There is the laying by of all the necessary materials. Not, he wrote (and Goldberg went on typing), that here in London one is cut off from such supplies in the normal course of events, but that work cannot begin until one knows one will not have to bother with such things, for a while at least. It is not a question, he wrote, of drawing up an inventory of all that is required, because that suggests that one can know exactly what will be required. Everything possible must be done, he wrote, and yet it must be as though nothing had been done. For unless there is the sense that nothing has been done there will be no work. And yet, unless everything has in fact been done, there will also be no work. Without the materials, he wrote, without the paints and the brushes, the pencils and the paper, above all without the panels of glass, there could have been no beginning, and I want to record here, wrote Harsnet (typed Goldberg), that there was a beginning, at 5.30 p.m. on Thursday 27 July 1967. I do not mean to imply, he wrote, that nothing existed before that moment, no plans, no designs, no sketches and no notes, of course there were plans and designs, sketches and notes, how could there not be, he wrote, when my whole life has been nothing but a preparation for this beginning, not only in the sense that everyone's life is always a preparation for every beginning in that life but in the quite specific sense that my own life has always been a preparation for this beginning, nothing but a preparation for this beginning, both consciously and unconsciously, with everything I have done as well as everything I have thought, everything I have felt as well as everything I have suffered. Not that I wish to say, he wrote, that everything is inevitable, on the contrary, I wish to assert emphatically that nothing is inevitable and nothing was inevitable, neither what I did nor what I thought, neither what I felt nor what I suffered, yet everything was necessary, a necessary beginning and necessary

11

to the beginning. Though to speak of beginning, wrote Harsnet (typed Goldberg) is misleading, since it was only after I had begun that I knew I had begun, while before I had begun, before the 27 July 1967, there was no beginning, as there was no end, there was no time and there was no freedom from time, only endless cups of coffee, endless cups of tea, endless biscuits and endless bacon sandwiches. Endless, he wrote, because I could see no end to them and because I could envisage no beginning. Endless, he wrote, because without hope. There is hope, he wrote, where there is making, and there is no hope where there is no making. There is no hope, he wrote, where there is no possibility of going wrong, where you can unthink in the afternoon what you have thought in the morning, think back in the evening what you have unthought in the afternoon. *Senza speme vivemo in disio*, he wrote, the saddest line ever written. I am not suggesting, he wrote, that this period was particularly unpleasant. It was neither pleasant nor unpleasant, though the endless peeing, he wrote, the endless getting up in the middle of the night when the ice clung to the window-panes and the taps were frozen, that was more unpleasant than pleasant, but it was not that, he wrote, these things will not change, my bladder will not improve and next winter the ice will still cling to the panes and the taps will still freeze, but I will not notice them. I will get up and pee once every two or three hours, as I have always done, but then I will return to my bed and sleep, I will return to my room and work. It is only during the time of waiting, wrote Harsnet, during the time without hope, that these things assume significance, only during the time without hope that one is conscious of them, that one remembers them with despair, that one anticipates them with dread. But I do not mean to suggest either, he wrote, that it was all waiting and no doing, all sitting and no action, for though it was impossible to tell when the beginning would come, indeed, he wrote, there could not have been a real beginning if it had been possible to tell, for if it had been possible to tell that would have meant that there had already been a beginning,

12

no, wrote Harsnet (typed Goldberg), occasionally things were done, work was begun, though it was soon abandoned, it added up to nothing, it only showed me that I had been mistaken in thinking that I had indeed started. In my own case, he wrote, and I can speak only for myself, in my own case and in my own life there have been very few genuine beginnings, only three or perhaps four. There was the revulsion at the fluidity of life and the first tube of paint, the revulsion at the meticulousness of painting with a brush and the first pot of paint, the revulsion at the viscousness of paint and the first readymade, the revulsion at the arbitrariness of the readymades and the first use of glass. Perhaps, he wrote, that is enough for a lifetime. Four real beginnings, wrote Harsnet, and four real rejections: the rejection of a life without art, the rejection of art, the rejection of any form of making, and the final rejection of all absolutes and the acceptance of compromise. Four beginnings, he wrote, each prompted by a sense of revulsion. *Four beginnings*, scribbled Goldberg in the margin of his typescript, *four revulsions*. So that behind the changes of direction, wrote Harsnet (typed Goldberg), this has always been a constant, the feeling of disgust in the pit of the stomach. I have often tried to describe it to myself, he wrote, but never with much success. For when it comes it is more violent, more annihilating, more interminable than I can remember it, this feeling in the pit of the stomach, this physical pain and physical desire to retch, to want to get rid of something, of everything, to want to make all that is inside emerge and disappear, drain away, mingle with the rest of the detritus of the world, but it is not only physical, a physical sensation, he wrote, it is physical but it is also something else, not moral, not psychological, not spiritual, but something else, something other than the purely physical. Nor is this feeling only provoked by the sight or the thought of art, he wrote. I also experienced it (it came upon me) when I signed the marriage register as well as when I saw the pig slaughtered. That is a fact, he wrote (and Goldberg typed), one of the few facts I can swear to, though I find it impossible to explain. And it

13

has to be said, he wrote, that its opposite, a feeling of elation, equally physical, equally extra-physical, has also been a constant feature of my life, manifesting itself regularly though impossible to predict, a feeling in the chest this time, the chest and perhaps the throat, a feeling of the heart leaping and the blood pumping, it came when I first took up a brush and made a mark on paper, it came when I picked up the first readymade and felt it transformed by that very action, it came when Madge rang to say she could not go on, when Annie wrote to say she was not coming back, when the idea of the glass first popped into my head. So, wrote Harsnet, there is continuity as well as discontinuity, but that does not mean, he wrote, that there exists what is called character, personality, *character*, Goldberg wrote in the margin, *personality*, as they seem to think, wrote Harsnet (and Goldberg went on typing), when they say you have such a generous character if you would only recognize it, or you have so much to offer, or it is not for myself I speak but for you, not for myself I mourn but for the waste of all that generosity, when they pour those words over you, character, generosity, warmth, looking sad, shedding tears, putting on a brave face, saying don't pay any attention to me, or, it's nothing, forget it, I'm crying for the waste, meaning waste if it's not directed towards them, but you have only to see what happens when one lets oneself be persuaded by that sort of thing, wrote Harsnet, you have only to see what happened to Hutchinson, MacMahon, Rollins and Goldberg. Taken in by the image of yourself they present you with, wrote Harsnet, instead of waiting in patience for the beginning, instead of waiting and then beginning, though beginning, having begun, he wrote, is not everything, is far from everything. It is quite possible, he wrote, that it will lead nowhere, even when one has begun at the right time in the right spirit, or at least not at the wrong time, in the wrong spirit, with the wrong plans and having made the wrong preparations, with the wrong tools and the wrong principles, on the wrong surface and with the wrong conception. Though it may well be, he wrote, that one actually achieves more working with the wrong plans and in the wrong spirit, with the wrong tools and the wrong principles, on the wrong surface and with the wrong conception, it may well be, he wrote (and Goldberg typed), that one achieves more than working with the right plans and in the right spirit, with the right tools and the right principles, on the right surface and with the right conception, though right and wrong and more and less are relative concepts and what seems right at one moment to one person may seem wrong at the same moment to another person or at another moment to the same person, and what seems more to one person at one moment may seem less to another person at the same moment or at another moment to the same person, *right, wrong, more, less, relative concepts*, scribbled Goldberg, in the margin, panting slightly as he bent over his old Olivetti portable, there is only the beginning, wrote Harsnet, or rather, there is only having begun, *beginning*, scribbled Goldberg, aware now of the black stains on his hands left by the felt-tip pen, *having begun*, there is only the feeling in the pit of the stomach or the feeling in the chest, wrote Harsnet, the feeling of sickness or the feeling of elation, those are not relative, he wrote, those are absolute. Yet is it possible to assert, he wrote, that work done with a lifting of the heart is better than work done with a contracting of the stomach? No, he wrote, it is not possible. It is only possible to assert that work begun with a lifting of the heart is likely to go on for longer than work begun with a contracting of the stomach, that work done with a lifting of the heart will develop further than work done with a contracting of the stomach, but there is nothing to indicate that the small amount of work which is the result of a contracting of the stomach will not be better than the large amount of work done with a lifting of the heart, than the rich development which is the likely result of work undertaken with a lifting of the heart, always bearing in mind, wrote Harsnet, and Goldberg, poring over the pages covered in his friend's tiny handwriting, wiped the sweat from his forehead with his sleeve, glanced up at the sheet in his typewriter, always

15

bearing in mind, he typed (as Harsnet had written), that better and worse are relative terms, and that one man's better is another man's worse, one age's better is another age's worse, one civilization's better is another civilization's worse, *better, worse, relative values*, scribbled Goldberg in the margin, always bearing in mind, wrote Harsnet, that in the long run it all comes to the same thing, *long run*, scribbled Goldberg in the margin, *same thing*. But for us on earth, wrote Harsnet, the run is not long but short. We are here, he wrote, with our needs and desires. We are here, for a brief while, with our energies intact, our needs and desires. What is required, he wrote, is to find an outlet for those energies, for those needs and desires, so that they do not turn inward and rend you to pieces, an outlet, he wrote, but never to imagine that what we do is ever going to be an everlasting achievement. *Outlet*, scribbled Goldberg in the margin, *folly of belief in permanence*. The trouble is, wrote Harsnet, that if you start with this insight it is difficult to go on and then the energies, the needs and desires, turn inward and eat you up. On the other hand, he wrote, if you don't see this clearly at the start you only produce more crap and there's enough in the world already. Honest crap you can flush down the lavatory, he wrote, but dishonest crap, of the kind produced by so-called artists, is more difficult to dispose of. Our civilization has at least this to its credit, he wrote, that it has found a way of rounding up this dishonest crap and incarcerating it in morgues, in fortified places with guards and alarm bells and the rest, thus keeping it off the streets, protecting decent citizens, and now, he wrote, there are even moves afoot to repel intruders by making them pay hard cash to enter these fortified places. It would have been simpler and more effective, he wrote, to lock the doors and seal up the entrances, simpler and more effective and cheaper than manning the whole building. But the shit proliferates, he wrote, and there is still much to be done. I myself am guilty, he wrote, in that I want the glass to be seen, I want it placed in a morgue and I want people to come in and see it, pay money and come in and see it, if needs be. First to make it, he wrote, and then to show it, and then to bring things to a finish. Those are the three steps, wrote Harsnet (typed Goldberg), first to make it, then to ensure that it is seen, and finally to finish with everything. Never in my life, he wrote, have I known so exactly what step to take after the step I am in the process of taking, and then what step to take after the step I will take after the step I am in the process of taking. Never before, he wrote, have I seen so clearly how to end. Now I have finally begun, he wrote, I have only to go on and the end will arrive. And to think, he wrote, that with all my previous work I barely knew what step to take first, let alone what step to take second, let us not talk about the third. Though it has to be said, he wrote, and Goldberg, his eye racing down the page covered in his friend's tiny handwriting, paused to sip from the glass of fresh orange-juice at his side, wiped his forehead and went on typing, it has to be said that I have occasionally had the illusion that I knew what step to take first and even, occasionally, what step to take second, I will not talk about a third. There is of course no logical reason why things should be different this time, wrote Harsnet, why this too should not be an illusion, the illusion of imagining that I know not only what step to take first but also what step to take second and even what step to take third. No logical reason, he wrote, but that will not make me change my plans once I have begun. Night, he wrote, work on the big glass and on the notes for the big glass, day, sleep and write this free-wheeling commentary on the entire project, viz. on the big glass and on the notes for the big glass. *Night*, scribbled Goldberg in the margin of his typescript, *work on glass, day, work on freewheeling commentary*. It is sometimes thought, wrote Harsnet (typed Goldberg) that, because there is no discernable principle of order in the universe or in our lives we should live in disorder. I, on the other hand, he wrote, have always held that precisely because there is no discernable principle of order in the universe or in our lives we should live in the greatest possible self-created

17

order. The greatest possible self-created order, he wrote, compatible of course with the freedom to work, which may mean very little order indeed or may mean a great deal of order, depending on the individual and the circumstances. It is up to each one of us, he wrote, at every point in our lives, to decide how much order and how much disorder, how much discipline and how much freedom we need for the best realization of our project of the moment, even though that project may turn out to be flawed or even utterly mistaken in the short run, of course I am only talking about the short run, he wrote, in the long run, as I have already said, both success and failure are quite without meaning, the notion of meaning is quite without meaning. *Long run*, wrote Goldberg in the margin, wiping the sweat from his forehead with his sleeve, *no meaning*. The real question, wrote Harsnet, is where the short run ends and the long run begins, since in the long run long and short are also without meaning. But that, he wrote, is part of what the big glass itself will try to explore, with its notion of delay. *Big glass*, wrote Goldberg in the margin, *delay*. That, wrote Harsnet, is part of the reason why I have chosen glass and not canvas or wood, that is why in my notes I have called it a delay in glass, which is to say a refusal of shit. I will perhaps call it a constipation in glass, wrote Harsnet, not a delay in glass, but an advance, he wrote, on my last ready-made, the hard stool, my present to Goldberg on the occasion of his third wedding. We will see, wrote Harsnet, whether he parts with it or not, whether his greed gets the better of his sentimentality. A project is a project, he wrote, and once it is begun it should be carried through to the end, regardless of doubts about meaning, doubts about long runs, or doubts about anything else, unless the body screams for you to stop, of course one cannot go on for long against the screaming of the body, but then that merely means one has miscalculated, it merely means one has begun too soon or too late or perhaps that the entire project was a miscalculation. That does not mean, he wrote, that if the body does not protest the project necessarily has any value, though

18

for reasons I have gone into already it is necessary to put such thoughts out of mind, they cannot help, they can only hinder, they cannot water, they can only blight. But it has to be said (it has to be said!) wrote Harsnet, and Goldberg, typing, smiled to himself, it has to be said, wrote Harsnet, that if every project is likely, if not certain, to result in the addition of a little more shit to the shit that already exists, there is also the possibility, faint it is true but real, of the unexpected, and this is what delay makes possible and what the onward rush of time, the ever-increasing acceleration of time, perpetually denies, and in addition to the possibility of the unexpected appearing in the coils of delay, in addition to that, it has to be said, he wrote, that whatever the project, however trivial, however exalted, it will always say more than its maker knows, and, if genuine (I will return to genuine), something will emerge which is distinct from whatever came before, from whatever elements went to make up the whole, a tone, a voice, which is not the tone or the voice of the maker but something else, something which, in my more optimistic moments, or perhaps my less clear-sighted moments, seems to be distinct from the shit though inseparable from it, a tone, a style, which links it to its maker's other genuine (I will return to genuine) productions. But just as the mere thought of the long run is liable to blight any work on which one is engaged, so the thought of a tone distinct from though inseparable from the shit is guaranteed to bring even the most promising project to a halt. We will leave it to Goldberg to disengage the tone from the shit, he wrote, we will leave it to Honeyman and McGough, much good may it do them, though I will no doubt come back to the question before my project is completed, the big glass and the notes to the big glass, these two to be worked on at night, and this freewheeling commentary on both to be written by day, putting down whatever comes into my head after a night's work, no correction, no revision, whatever comes into my head, the first two to be worked on by artificial light, the strategy clear, this by natural light wherever possible, no strategy at all, the first to be exhibited, the second to be published in the form of sheets in a box, a blue box or a red box, I have not yet made up my mind, in a limited edition, not a luxury edition but a restricted edition, five hundred boxes perhaps or even two hundred and fifty, all that will become clearer in the course of my work on the big glass, of my work on the notes to the big glass, now I have finally embarked on the major project of my life, the climactic project of my life, leading to the end of my life, all will grow clearer, wrote Harsnet, whether to try and call back and destroy all I have done till now or let it be, whether to burn this commentary or let it be, or perhaps leave it to Goldberg to do whatever he wants with, all these things will no doubt be resolved before the work is completed, that is the beauty of being in the middle of a project, that time itself, which had seemed such an enemy before I started, rushing forward and dragging me with it, impervious to my pleas, has suddenly turned friendly, flops down at my feet, licks my ankles, lets me know it is on my side. And how much more, wrote Harsnet, when the project on which you are engaged is the major project of your life, the project of your life. It is funny, wrote Harsnet (typed Goldberg), how reluctant I was to say anything like that here in the first few days, how instinctively I felt it might endanger the entire project, how everything might collapse around me the moment I said that. It must be a measure of my confidence, he wrote, that I can now say, in these notes, without any kind of trepidation, that this is the major project of my life, that beside it the rest pales into insignificance, if it was not insignificant anyway, beside it or anything else. Which is not to say, he wrote, that the present project has any value over and above the others, mine and those of everyone else, I have been into the question of value already and will not return to it now, has any value or that its outcome has any value, I have to repeat this, simply that now, for me, today, after the things I have done and given the time left me, it is the most important thing, it is what, from the time I first picked up a pencil and made a mark on a piece of paper, everything has logically led up to. I do not

20

want, wrote Harsnet, to try and trace this logic or to dwell, in these notes, on the nature and direction of my earlier work, especially, he wrote, as I have always held that any new work worth its salt should be essentially different from all that has gone before, all that others have done and all that you have done, just as the deeds of each new day must never simply repeat those of the previous day or days. Nevertheless, wrote Harsnet (typed Goldberg), I think that this needs saying, quite calmly and objectively, in this commentary, which will not spare me when I have done badly or in the wrong spirit or left half-done, but will not either, in a spirit of false modesty, gloss over those things in my life and work which have been a success, even, mildly, a triumph. And by this stage in this commentary, he wrote, there is no need to qualify the words success, triumph, and the rest, qualifications can be taken as read. Besides, he wrote, now that I am at last working on the big glass and have set up the two panels and locked them into their metal frame, notions like success and failure are no longer pertinent, there is only the project and its outcome, *project*, scribbled Goldberg in the margin, *outcome*, and words like success and failure can safely be left to others, wrote Harsnet. But that is not quite right either, he wrote. The fact is that the project itself will call into question the notion of success and failure, my theme in the big glass, he wrote, is, after all, the calling into question of such terms as success and failure, the calling into question of such notions as project and even work. The big glass and the notes for the big glass, he wrote, not the big glass by itself and the notes by themselves, the big glass and the notes for the big glass, the notes for the big glass and the big glass, he wrote, never the one alone or the other alone, for neither by itself has any meaning, neither by itself will have any force, but always both together, not as text and gloss, not as image and caption, but always as exchange and delay, mirror and reflection. The temptation of magic and mystery, he wrote. How often this century. Dali, he wrote. Roussel. Pessoa. But Dada opposite error. Anarchy no answer. Lucidity, he wrote.

21

Always lucidity. Even in the dissection of lucidity. Even in the undermining of lucidity. As in my little essay, *The Death of Images*. As in all I have ever attempted. That is why it is important to work at night, he wrote. Not to be warmed by the sun. Cold light of the fluorescent tube. No way of escape. Alone with the glass under the cold light. No thoughts. No feelings. No painterly skills. The hand moves. The eye measures. The hand picks up. Places. Basta. That is the point of the glass, he wrote. Not a surface to be covered. Not an object to be made. Not a picture of, he wrote, and not the thing itself. Shadow and projection, he wrote. Present and absent at the same time. Existent and non-existent. A shadow has to be cast by something, he wrote. Every shadow implies an object and a source of light. On the glass the shadow, but shadow of what? What will the viewer see? he wrote. Something on the glass. And the glass. And something through the glass. The wall of the gallery, the other exhibits hanging on it. People moving, standing, leaning forward. And his reflection. Himself bending forward and looking. Looking at. Looking through. Looking back at himself looking. *Shadow of what?* wrote Goldberg in the margin, cursing under his breath as his elbow dislodged the pile of typewritten sheets stacked on the desk beside the typewriter, tapping them back to neatness, wiping his brow with his sleeve, typing on. The assembled elements of the glass, he typed (as Harsnet had written). Bride above, bachelors below, cooler between them. Condemned never to meet. The gaze of the bachelors, wrote Harsnet. It strips her bare. She solicits the gaze, he wrote. And it leads to her flowering, to her escape from her condition. Glass as shadow of fourth dimension, he wrote. Patience, he wrote. Do not run ahead of yourself. Do not substitute the idea for the object. But do not fetishize the object either. Glass and box, he wrote. Box and glass. Leave explanations to Goldberg, he wrote. To Honeyman and McGough. To Goldman and Golding. To Pizzetti and Baiocchi. To Moss and McGrindle. Of course, he wrote (and Goldberg typed), there may be nothing to leave,

22

nothing to explain, nothing to understand, even though I have prepared long enough and only started when the time was ripe, even though I began full of confidence and managed to persuade myself, for a while, that I was well under way. But the fact of the matter is, he wrote, that none of it is right, or rather, that what has so far been accomplished is wrong and what has not yet been accomplished is only right because it has not yet had the chance to be proved wrong. 1 lb. tomatoes, he wrote, 1 cauliflower, 2 packs date biscuits, 1 pack butter, 1 lemon, 3 tins sardines, 1 tin tuna. Days getting perceptibly shorter, he wrote, nights colder. To clear the mind, he wrote (and Goldberg typed), to reach the peak, one last effort for one last time, one supreme effort, total concentration, and then the end. Maximum clarity, he wrote, for as long as it takes. Total elimination of all that is irrelevant, he wrote. Keep shit at bay, keep warmth at bay, those maggots of feeling, breeding in the shit, sooner or later it gets to them all, even Hilda, love at last, her very words, who would have thought it. Goldberg I had known it would attack, he wrote, and sooner rather than later, the soil was ripe for the sprouting of concern, refugees, famine, the bomb, you only had to look at him, sentiment inevitable, despite my efforts, despite my scorn. But Hilda, wrote Harsnet, a major disappointment. Love at last, so she said. At last? I said. At last? In the case of Goldberg, he wrote, unfortunate upbringing accounts for much. But no excuse for Hilda. I realized I had not been fair to myself. I realized I had not properly understood my own needs. I couldn't believe my ears but she repeated it: I realized I had not properly understood my own needs. The words of my sister, wrote Harsnet, a major disappointment. After that, what was there to say? After that, after those words, wrote Harsnet (and Goldberg typed), what possible relationship could exist between us? The comfort of having the big glass here at last, he wrote, of living in the shadow of its coldness, its emptiness. No Hildas. No Goldbergs. No words. Just the glass. Cold to the touch. Cold to look at. Peace. First the glass, he wrote, and then the show and finally the end.

23

Not forgetting the notes in the blue box, he wrote, number the slips perhaps or leave unnumbered, each slip to record date and place of purchase of one element of the glass, size and shape and substance before incorporation, brief history of its purchase, tube ticket, bus ticket, receipt, weather on day of purchase and weather on day of incorporation, temperature on day of purchase and temperature on day of incorporation, 1 tin peaches, bread, marmite (small), remember laundry, one day like any other (and Goldberg, pausing in his typing, picked up his pen and put a small question mark in the margin of his typescript and then carried on), now winter has come, but every night like every other, walking round the glass under the cold light, measuring the glass, preparing the glass. Time will only enter where I want it, wrote Harsnet. An artefact is lost in its timelessness, he wrote. The pretence that this is not so is what makes me sick, he wrote, when I look at the works of the past. The pretence that it exists in your time and my time. If the glass has any virtue at all, he wrote, it is that it refuses to pretend. If it has to tell a story, he wrote, it will be the story of the machine inside the ghost, of the ghost animated by the machine. And us? he wrote. Desiring machines. Nothing more, nothing less. Thus glass perhaps not too far from old realism. Female suspended in non-space in top panel, he wrote. Bachelors strung together like pegs on a line on lower panel. They can never touch, he wrote, yet act upon each other from their separate worlds. The machine does not function, he wrote. The desired outcome is delayed. Does that mean that one day it will happen? Or is the delay perpetual? And yet, he wrote, the impact of the whole must be that of a storm. A hurricane. *Storm*, scribbled Goldberg in the margin. *Hurricane*. The time for gentle breezes is over, wrote Harsnet (and Goldberg typed), the time for the oohs and ahs, for the oh so beautiful and the ah so expressive, for the deep humanity and the flesh-coloured tints, for the sensitive and the profound, for the exquisite and the brilliant. Nothing but a hurricane will do now, he wrote. It must be impossible to stand up against it, he wrote, impossible to draw breath before it. It must knock your legs from under you, pound the breath from your body. No more learned monographs from Sweeney and McGough, he wrote, from Pizzetti and Baiocchi, from Goldman and Golding, from Rosenblum and Honeyman. No more notes, he wrote, no more queries, no more space in the work of X and time in the work of Y, no more symbolism, no more allegory, no more influence of X and legacy of Y, no more background and no more foreground, no more social this and political that, no more Heidegger and no more Heisenberg, no more still life and no more portraiture, no more collage and no more frottage, no more lines and no more surfaces, no more genius and no more talent, no more creation and no more mechanical reproduction, no more African masks and no more Cycladic figures, no more clowns and no more nudes, no more museums, no more galleries, no more group shows, no more one-man shows, no more public commissions, no more prizes, no more shit and no more vomit. It is not, wrote Harsnet (typed Goldberg), that I am under any illusion on this score. There will of course always be critics and there will always be oohs and ahs, there will always be shit and there will always be vomit. I exaggerate, he wrote. There will not always be critics and the rest, just as there will not always be man and the rest. But they will be there for long enough, long enough. I am under no illusion on that score, he wrote, I am under no illusion that the big glass will in an instant blow all that away, flatten the critics against the walls, tear paintings from their places, bring the galleries tumbling to the ground. Nor am I under the illusion that I alone am free of illusion. But that is the effect, he wrote, that is the effect I am aiming at. Cold cold cold but with the impact of a hurricane. That is the effect. First the making of the glass, he wrote, then the showing of the glass, and finally the end. Leave this notebook in the safe keeping of Goldberg? he wrote. Or destroy? See how it goes, he wrote. I am under no illusion as to effect, he wrote. But the aim must be high, extreme. Infinite slimness, he wrote. Picture as infinite slimness. Not so glass. For glass no longer surface

25

of infinite slimness but shadow of fourth dimension, seen by us as three, reproduced as two. Shadow of another world, he wrote, and Goldberg, picking up his pen, wiping his forehead, wrote in the margin, *infinite slimness, fourth dimension*. 2 packs date biscuits, wrote Harsnet, 2 avocados, 1 cauliflower, 6 eggs (fr.r.), 1 lb. onions, 1 lettuce (cos), 1 bag oranges, 1 pack sugar, 1 pack salt. Projection of another dimension or dimensions as when the sun breaks through a cloud and washing-up powder, launderette, what else was Jacob's ladder? he wrote, and Goldberg, staring at his friend's manuscript all those years later, typed that in and put a little question mark in the margin of his typescript. Before 1500 possible to put ladder into image, wrote Harsnet (typed Goldberg), no longer so now. Shadow of ladder yes, ladder no. Dali's error. Why he remains a mere titillator. Magritte closer but still too clever. Subject too important for tricks. Magritte like man who learns to somersault backwards from standing position and keeps on doing it. You begin by admiring but it soon grows boring. So Harsnet. And Goldberg, pushing the sweat out of his eyes with the sleeve of his pullover, grabbed the pen and put another question mark in the margin by the whole passage. Magritte, like Dali, wants you to admire him, wrote Harsnet (and Goldberg, laying the pen aside, began to type again). Nobody to be admired when big glass shown, he wrote. Not admiration but anxiety, wonder, disgust, terror. Shadow of Other, he wrote, reflection of spectator, window onto room behind. On the glass or in the glass? he wrote. You lean forward to see more clearly and see only your own reflection. Come too close and you lose it altogether. As for Diana, the arrival of Actaeon in the cave the beginning of the end. All *Metamorphosis* about Narcissus, he wrote. Ovid by the Black Sea, cut off from native speech, he wrote. Mind of Antaeus remains unchanged, he wrote. That is the horror. *Mens tantum pristina mansit*. And Goldberg, pushing back his chair, stepping over the piles of papers and magazines littering the floor of his study, scanned the bookcase, found what he wanted, brought the book back to his

26

desk, licked his middle finger and turned the pages, found the passage and copied carefully into the margin: *only his mind remains unchanged*. The whole world changes but your mind does not, wrote Harsnet (and Goldberg typed). Kafka's *Metam*, he wrote, *The Death of Ivan Ilych*. Metam as delay, he wrote. The beauty of glass, he wrote. You are forced to ask: Do I stop here or do I go on through? Christ as mediator in older art, he wrote. Romantic desire for unmediated world. Anxiety of Friedrich leads to anxiety of Schoenberg, anxiety of Wordsworth leads to anxiety of Stevens. Eradicate anxiety, he wrote, and Goldberg, in the margin, *anxiety*. Eradicate anxiety in the image, wrote Harsnet (and Goldberg typed), for that leads to contentment in the spectator. Substitute anxiety in the spectator, he wrote, brought about by nothing other than the apparent lack of anxiety in the image. In an anxious world serenity as cause of heightened anxiety, he wrote, and Goldberg, seizing his felt-tip pen, bent over the typewriter and wrote in the margin *anxiety? serenity?* Anxiety will get you nowhere, wrote Harsnet. Anxiety no guarantee of authenticity. The right conditions for serenity, he wrote. Laundry! he wrote in the margin of his page, and Goldberg, after a moment's hesitation, typed it in and added, in brackets, *margin!* Romanticism, he wrote, not a wet Romanticism. Wet R as (half-hearted) belief that energy equals salvation, he wrote. There is no answer, he wrote, because there is no question. *No answer*, scribbled Goldberg in the margin of his typescript, *because no question*. He dropped the pen and went on typing. Dada as despair, he typed. So Swiss. So Protestant. Despair as despair at lack of salvation, wrote Harsnet. But salvation from what? What we have is *all* we have, he wrote. Why this need to nudge the world into being other than it is? he wrote. Goldberg and his books. Hilda and her lovers. Always the same old story. You inhabit a world without hope, she says to me. Such coldness, she says. I shiver in your presence. Such heat, I tell her. I watch you fizzle and burn. Fire, she tells me, has always been a source of goodness. Think of a piece of paper, I tell her. Watch it burn and smoulder, crinkle and turn to ashes, leaving nothing but a stink behind. To think that the self-same parents could have given birth to the two of us, she says. Self-same! Who says self-same any more? Help me, she says. I'm so unhappy. And Goldberg too: Help me, I'm so unhappy. What do they want me to do? Blow their noses for them? And why me? Why me? Distinguish between energy and passion, he wrote. Do not be taken in by current usage. Clarify, he wrote. Clarify, clarify. Do not stop. What looks like a dead end may only be the result of personal weakness. The bachelors, he wrote. Policeman, judge, delivery boy, priest, referee, commissionaire. The uniform is the man, he wrote. Uniform as sign of virile youth, he wrote. Women and uniforms, he wrote. Anna and Vronsky. Bachelor society. Rites of passage. Man with dog at launderette, he wrote. How dog leapt onto one of the machines and curled up there. Nippy little feller, man said. I agreed. He offered me a cigarette. I declined. Won't let me out of his sight for a minute, he said. Not since the missus died. I helped him fold his sheets. He let them trail on the ground. Filth at the edges. He didn't notice. Dog waited till we were done, then jumped off. C'mon you, he said, and held the door open for him. Dog at his heels as he went off down the road. Diana, he wrote (and Goldberg typed). Melampus. Ichnobates. Pamphagus. The wooded vale. The spring. The cave. Right hand side still too empty, he wrote. The mechanical Diana, he wrote. Difficulty of devising a structure that will stand firm yet will not be over-heavy, he wrote. Difficulty of welding glass to metal frame. Calamity if glass breaks. And if it topples over it certainly will. Last ten days trying to devise way to stabilize frame, he wrote. Always a solution, only a question of finding it, he wrote. Hadn't reckoned with weight of glass in my cal-culations. Check Higinbothams, he wrote. Last night almost a disaster, he wrote. Difficult to stay calm, he wrote. With panels of glass this size in such a small room bound to be problems. Yet I like it like that. I like the sense of its filling the room and yet also, in a way, of its being non-existent. I have always liked to work in a simple room, he wrote. A natural part of a house. No fuss. Bare boards. Bare walls. Naked bulb or neon lighting. Studios for the production of art-crap, he wrote. Studios nothing but shit-houses. I have never been in the business of producing art-crap, he wrote. Except perhaps at the start. No excuse then except age. And the fact that I soon got away from it. No virtue attached to that though. Simply the sense of physical disgust which filled me whenever I took up a brush and dipped it in paint. So strong that merely stopping was no solution. Desire to make, he wrote, but physical revulsion at the falsity of all making. Had to satisfy that desire, he wrote, yet find a way of doing so that would not have that physical effect on me. The history of art, he wrote, is the history of dead-ends transformed into springboards. What's the matter with me? wrote Harsnet (typed Goldberg). What am I doing pontificating about art and history? That too is crap, he wrote, though harmless crap. Yet who would have thought I would talk to myself in this way in these notes? he wrote. Is it because the right hand side is going so badly? Too much there or too little? Something is missing, he wrote. I need to introduce a different dimension and I am at a loss. Have been for over a week. Rang Danny and he said to come round. Good game, usual outcome. Beat back a pawn storm on Queen side and eventually turned it round. His attacks always violent but uncoordinated. Contrived elegant check on the hour. But it did nothing for the glass. Same problem, same lack of ideas. Boiled cauliflower. Struck as always by its resemblance to human brain. Very tasty as salad, lemon dressing. The joys of false analogies, he wrote. Of the almost precise correspondences. Jake. And how upset they were when he took off his hat and smiled. A very pleasing day. And Goldberg, pushing the typewriter to one side, seized his pen and pad and wrote: Jake. What happened was this. Harsnet was due to get married. The date was fixed. I was best man. All waited in registry office. Where was H? Eventually he arrived, with minutes to spare, wearing a ridiculous sort of check hat. Nobody said anything. Then, just before stepping up to sign the register, he took off his hat. His hair was bright red instead of H's black. We all looked again and it wasn't H. The bastard had met this Jake a year or two back and at once noted the resemblance. Kept in touch with him, waiting for the right occasion to use him. He was quite frank about the whole thing, told us H. had given him a fiver to turn up, asked Madge if she wanted to go through with it, which of course she didn't. Her father furious. Herself in tears. When I got back home there was H., in the living-room, pleased as Punch. Write up? wrote Goldberg. Appendix? Or note at foot of page? He pushed the pad aside, drew the typewriter towards him and began to type again, squinting down at his friend's tiny handwriting. I hear about these artists, so-called, he typed (as Harsnet had written), who work all day and all night, whose work is their passion. Paint all over their clothes, all over the studio, external mark of intrinsic worth. I sometimes feel sorry, wrote Harsnet (typed Goldberg), that I am not of their kind. That I grow bored after an hour or two. That I can do most of my work in my suit without getting dirty. If they are looking for salvation, he wrote, they will find it. How easy to rest in the bosom of the Lord, he wrote. Worthy men, he wrote, full of the mystery and importance of their Calling. On the other hand, he wrote, there are people like Goldberg, like Moss and McGrindle, who believe in nothing, except perhaps in personal power and glory, though they would like to believe in something 'higher'. I frankly do not know which I prefer, wrote Harsnet. Sometimes I think the latter, sometimes the former. Do I have to choose between goat's cheese and chocolate cake? as Queneau used to ask. It is the right hand side on both panels that is worrying me, he wrote. Nothing has gone right on that side from the moment I began. I need to move slowly across from the left and see where things start to go wrong, he wrote. Except that I cannot work like that. I have made my plans and I must stick to them. Even in the plan, though, I now realize, he wrote, there was a certain vagueness about the right hand side of both panels.

Perhaps because in painting as in writing we start from top left hand side, so that the right is always less clear. Interesting to examine the old masters from that point of view, he wrote. However, he wrote, for that very reason, the right hand side should have been even more solid, even more thought through than the left. But there it is, he wrote. The plans are made, work has begun, there is no going back. Work as the fancy takes me, he wrote. A little bit here, a little bit there. Wherever there is interest on the day in question. The absurd idea, he wrote, that a work of art grows from nothing into something, from acorn into oak. Fostered by illusion of paint, which spreads out over the surface. I want to pick up and put down, he wrote, not spread out in gooey mass. Simple elements, he wrote, complex whole. Infinitely simple elements, infinitely complex whole. Yet retain even in final product sense of simplicity of elements, of possibility of dismantling. Penny my heroine, he wrote. Weave through the day, unweave at night. Give each viewer the chance to do just that. Each element, he wrote, must be honest, and Goldberg, in the margin, *each element: honest.* He pulled the notebook towards him and wrote: Check early drypoint, *Heroin for a Penny*, refs. Penelope. He pushed the pad aside, took a sip of orange juice, wiped his forehead, and went on typing. No element, he typed (as Harsnet had written) should ever pretend to be more or less than itself. No mystery, wrote Harsnet (typed Goldberg), no magic. Big glass like big engine. You will enter my machine, he wrote, and the trip will consist in the discovery that we cannot even get started. Desire alone never enough to get machine started, he wrote. Desire never enough to confer meaning where there was none, to transform simple elements into work of art. Into Work of Art. *Desire*, scribbled Goldberg in the margin. *Machine.* Remember All-Bran, wrote Harsnet, remember milk. And Goldberg, pulling the pad towards him and seizing his felt-tip pen, began to write. Dear Harsnet, he wrote, you may keep your door closed and not answer when I ring the bell, you may refuse to answer my letters or return my calls when I leave a message

31

on your answering machine, but sooner or later we are
bound to meet and this time I will not let you fob me off
with a smile. Dear Harsnet, he wrote, you have been seen
doing circuit training with Korchnoi and the Brighton and
Hove Albion football team. If I am to do what you asked,
he wrote, you will have to co-operate. We will have to meet
and discuss some of the problems. He pushed the pad aside
and began to type again. There are those who imagine, he
typed (as Harsnet had written), that because they know the
machine will not start they can afford to ignore it. But what
if the motorless machine is what it is all about? Goldberg,
pushing back the typewriter and drawing the pad towards
him, began again. Dear Harsnet, he wrote, you may be
amused to hear that one of my sons spotted you the other
day training with Korchnoi and the Brighton and Hove
Albion football team. We all knew of your friendship with
Korchnoi, he wrote, how could we not, the papers have
been so full of it. We have also followed his preparations
for the world title bout with Karpov, some of us, it must
be confessed, with a certain amount of incredulity, since,
however much these world championship matches are now
dependent on stamina rather than brilliance, it has struck
more than a few people that a chess player is not a footballer,
in particular a fifty-year-old self-exiled Russian Grandmaster is not a footballer, and that to think that by training
like one he will become as fit is not only an illusion, it is a
dangerous illusion. Besides, wrote Goldberg, you have only
to see where Brighton are placed in the League to wonder
at the wisdom of associating with them in any capacity.
Even so, he wrote, what might, *à la rigueur*, be acceptable
for a Russian Grandmaster seems merely perverse in a retired
artist. However, wrote Goldberg, turning the page and tearing it slightly in his eagerness to go on, my son is rather
short-sighted, something he has inherited from his mother,
and recently, during a school trip to Dieppe, he dropped
his glasses and cracked one of the lenses. He is also prone
to jump to conclusions. So it may not, after all, have been
you he saw. In which case forgive me for writing as I have

32

done. He pushed the pad aside, took out his handkerchief and wiped his face, stuffed the handkerchief back in his pocket and began to type again. Desire, he typed (as Harsnet had written), a most boring subject. Yet, wrote Harsnet, I keep coming back to it. The question, he wrote, is how to make desire interesting. Even amusing. If my lady can be said to be amusing. For more and more she is coming to resemble a mechanical praying mantis, frozen there in the glass, he wrote. Colour not yet quite right, he wrote. Need more silver, more white. But something is happening in that upper panel. More than can be said for the lower one, he wrote. Though distinctions between the two growing more apparent. Precise definition, clear articulation, accurate perspective below, he wrote (and Goldberg typed), fluidity, flatness, cloudiness above. The big glass as the end of art, he wrote. No point in not being ambitious. Though ambition has been the grave of many minor artists, it is also that without which no artist can be called major – with all the provisos about art, artists, major, minor, already touched on. There is a point in everyone's life, he wrote, when all caution must, as they say, be thrown to the winds, all doubts stilled, when the most extreme risks have to be taken. It is the moment, he wrote, when a man suddenly realizes that there is no tomorrow, no second chance, only today, this chance, now. Is this the moment of truth, he wrote, or the greatest temptation? I have been preparing myself for this for the whole of my life, he wrote. I can say without embarrassment that I have been training for this for a long time, that I have learned to breathe the rarefied air, that I now know when to stand still and when to move forward, when to attack and when to retreat, when to leave a problem to resolve itself and when to go on working at it till the solution emerges. I have learned to keep going, wrote Harsnet (typed Goldberg), even when the voices scream at me to stop, to lie down, to turn to something else. Blake, he wrote, If a fool persist in his folly, etc. I have also learned, he wrote, to heed the voices when necessary. Though it is never possible to be sure one is doing the right thing, he wrote. There are always moments of doubt. After the initial impetus has run out, he wrote, and before one has got in so far that it is easier to finish than to go back, it is then that it becomes hard to be sure of your footing, hard to know why you are doing what you are doing, hard to know if you are doing correctly what you are doing. That is why so few books on the middle game, he wrote, though plenty on openings and endgames. None of that would of course be comprehensible to Moss and McGrindle, he wrote, to Pizzetti and Baiocchi, to Goldman and Goldstein, though Goldberg, to his credit, has had an inkling, has to some extent faced the thought that he might be wasting his whole life, for that's what it comes down to in the end, he wrote, wasting a whole life when something useful might have been salvaged, something valuable perhaps, it is the refusal of those alternatives that occasionally makes one shiver. One? wrote Harsnet (typed Goldberg). The darkness? Well well well, he wrote. Do not retreat into irony, he wrote. One last thought on the subject and then basta: they – Moss and McGrindle, etc. – imagine that something drives one on, a clear vision, that one knows what one is doing. The difficulty is that it does not, one does not – not in one's art, not in one's life. Yet one grows restless doing nothing. Scratching one's balls. So where does the desire to be up and doing come from? Too complicated, he wrote. All there in the big glass anyway, let others tease it out. Keep going, he wrote. Buy shirt. Bulb. Establish rhythm. The density of the glass, he wrote. The intractability of the glass. Have to get to grips with what this does to the image. Its refusal to respond, as canvas and paper respond. Tried projecting negative of Bride from holograph enlarger, he wrote, but image thin and weak where I want it strong (though indeterminate). Near asphyxiation last night, he wrote. Acid. Try fuse wire. I sometimes think, he wrote, that if in one sense I am back in the nursery trying to make a big toy with nothing but wood and string, in another I am back in the classroom fiddling with bunsen burners while Mr Alexander walks round sniffing with his long distinguished nose in the air. And playing in the mud, kicking a ball, he wrote. What greater happiness than that? It is a matter of finding out how to adapt, he wrote. How to keep doing what one enjoyed doing as a child but adapting it to the changing circumstances. Bless relaxes, he wrote, roll down the socks. Paz visit yesterday, dinner McVittie's, wrote Harsnet. Excellent meal. Gave me first edition of Alekhine's *Best Games* picked up in Delhi. In his usual fine form, doing 1003 things. Invited me to his reading tomorrow, I drew the line at that. We walked till 3 a.m., Embankment, West End, Soho, he talked of India, temple sculpture, smell, then of Breton, Lévi-Strauss, Soupault, interconnection between Surrealism and ethnography in France between the wars, Mexico, death, Leiris, Roussel, etc. After India, Poland, Munich, quick trip to Milan to see Berio and Eco, Paris, Queneau unwell, Butor planning book on Diabelli Variations, that man is an interpretative machine, Paz said, whatever you feed him he devours in a few months and a year later out comes a book. Always a masterpiece of criticism, empathy. A mind that can turn faster and keep going longer than that of anyone I know, so Paz, wrote Harsnet. He is in a class by himself, Paz said. The rest of us are running a different race – by choice perhaps. In Munich, Paolozzi, more like a Minotaur than ever, obsessed now with plaster casts. Also Beuys, passing through, hat and horse, quite mad. He sent me a card, Paz said, just one line, Did Dada do dis or did e do dat? I wrote back, Paz said, I told him, Dada dead as dodo eat your hat. He hadn't, Paz said. Not when I saw him. It was still on his head. I told him, wrote Harsnet (typed Goldberg) it was people like him who kept the idea of art going, kept the opera houses of the world open, kept the bookshops of the world open, they ought to take you out and shoot you, I said to him. They tried, he said. If you came from Mexico, he said, you would give up this shallow cynicism and understand just how important it is to keep the bookshops open, to keep the galleries open, even to keep the opera houses open. The trouble with you is, he said, that you've grown fat in your little cocoon here in London, cut off from the realities of

35

the world. He knows I never argue, so he left off and praised the food. We finished up on the track. At least the telly hasn't yet cottoned on to the dogs, I told him, but he said in Mexico it had. Backed Tiny Thomas and took home £4. Did you know, Paz asked me, that Thomas Aquinas was only four foot ten? I didn't. His collected works, he said, probably fill four foot ten of shelf space. All written by hand by candlelight. We embraced. When I got back I sat in front of the big glass with the door shut and the lights off, till dawn. Something missing lower right hand side. Keyhole to peep through? But what if glass breaks as I make it? Paint hole on glass and charge to see through? Here Prospero discovers Ferdinand and Miranda playing at chess. A most high miracle. A magic peep-hole, wrote Harsnet. Pay extra and you may see Ferdinand and Miranda playing at chess. Or you may see exactly what you would see by looking through the glass at any point. No, he wrote. Escape from myth. Escape from the literary. Big glass as machine for shredding myths. The Shredder of Myths or Delay in Glass. And Goldberg, in the margin: *The Shredder of Myths or Delay in Glass*. It is growing tedious, wrote Harsnet (typed Goldberg). I am growing tired of it, he wrote. That is how Autumn affects me. The burning of the leaves. The shortening of the days. My ideal home, he wrote: no trees, no sky with fleeting clouds. Underground car-park perhaps? The car-park as the death of nostalgia, he wrote. We will not have got rid of nostalgia, he wrote, till we have got rid of the sky. Socks, he wrote. Shirt. 6 eggs (fr.r.). Cauliflower. Bread. 1 pack butter. Marmalade. It is all a question, he wrote, of what we owe ourselves. Do I owe it to myself to finish? How deep is my boredom? Is it stronger than my desire to complete what I have begun? And if stronger does that mean truer? What does true mean? What does strong mean? What is the real temptation, he wrote, to stop or to go on? Show up the vagaries of causality, he wrote, the banalities of style. Show up the folly of I feel this so I do that. There is a story, he wrote, there is a story that is being told. Somehow. Somewhere. Its shadow passes across the glass. The story of desire and its non-fulfilment. Of the lack of relation between cause and effect. Do not tell the story, he wrote. Show the smile by which we respond to the story. The Cheshire Cat. More important even than Humpty Dumpty for understanding last hundred years, he wrote. The Big Glass as Cheshire Cat. That is only another way of saying Frozen Hurricane, he wrote. Sense that this is now or never time, he wrote. And yet, if I fail, it is only a failure. Only? he wrote. Only? In other words, he wrote, am I right or wrong to see this as decisive? Is that an insight into how things really are, or only one more passing thought? My plans have been well laid, he wrote. The project is well under way. There is no reason to fail. Sitting with the curtains open and the moon shining in on the barely begun big glass, he wrote, sitting keeping vigil with it all night after my walk with Paz, I was afraid. Partly a question of its size, of the intractability of the glass, of its icy self-containment. Sense of my own helplessness in relation to it, he wrote. Also, he wrote, it repels me. It not only frightens me, it repels me. Cold glass and cold metal frame filling that room. I did not know what to do with it, why I was there. I felt it annihilating me. I felt its coldness spreading through my body, killing off the cells, one by one. And yet, wrote Harsnet (typed Goldberg), I also knew that it was this cold that drew me, this steady destruction of body and imagination, this utter alienness, as though only that could still excite me, as though anything less alien would only leave me indifferent. Not easy though, he wrote, to submit oneself to it, to enter its orbit. Always the danger of the cold spreading too fast, of my not being able to live with it. And then, he wrote, there is the question of why that dread should also be a source of excitement. Is it because one does not turn to art for comfort? For safety? Because if you want comfort and safety you keep well away from art? From real art? You only turn to it as people climb mountains and cross deserts – to find out what you are made of by doing what you hardly dare to do. But is that an answer? And what kind of answer is it? A long night, he wrote. I got up occasionally and touched the cold glass. Touched the metal frame. Leaned my forehead against it. Then returned to my chair. Moonlight, he wrote. Bare boards. Glass gleaming. I kept my eyes on it the whole time, he wrote. Nothing visible on its surface, only the cold gleam. As if all the work of the past four months had only been a dream, the cutting and the drilling, the painting, the moulding of the lead wire. All a dream and the glass was as smooth and blank as when I first installed it. Like cutting into the surface of a pond, I thought, wrote Harsnet (typed Goldberg), like pressing paint onto the surface of a pond, with total concentration and total folly. That is perhaps the point of the big glass, wrote Harsnet. That it is like the mind itself. Work on it is like a dream, or like thoughts of what a work would be like. Yet at the same time there is work done upon it, he wrote, and which remains, as it does not in the mind. Yet it was as though that night, in the moonlight, in the silence, as though even the work, the months of steady labour, had only been an illusion, only the dream of work, the dream of progress, and I had not even begun and never would begin, though at different moments in my life I might have had the illusion that I had begun and even, perhaps, finished. And yet, wrote Harsnet, it is this which excites me, this which makes me want to go on. As if my whole life, he wrote, had been spent working at the glass and at the same time had been spent doing nothing at all. As if even my memories of work on the glass were not memories but fantasies and fancies. They say that at the moment of death the whole of one's past life flashes before one's eyes. I doubt it. But what if at the moment of birth the whole of one's life to come were to flash before one's eyes and then to be immediately wiped away, forgotten, while we laboriously go through all the pleasures and sorrows, all the hopes and frustrations that make up a life, meeting people and parting from them, listening to them and speaking to them, to go through tasting all we taste in the course of our long lives, seeing all we see, every leaf at every moment and every cloud at every moment, and hearing

38

all we hear, the hooting of every car and the singing of every bird and every performance of the Brandenburg concertos, go through all that, in time, very slowly, though we had already been through it all, every moment of it, leaf, cloud, concerto, in one brief but intense instant, everything perfectly formed but over in less than a second? And the reverse of that, wrote Harsnet, the feeling that all we have already felt and seen and heard has yet to happen, is so far only a dream, a fantasy, and the sense, he wrote, that this may be a feeling we experience again and again throughout our lives, that the elements of experience have failed to catch on to the glass of our lives, or that the glass is there and waiting for the experience to be registered, that it can wait for ever, for it does not know the meaning of time. All that and more went through my mind, wrote Harsnet, as I sat there in the moonlight in the silence, but it was as if it was the glass which was telling me this, that the glass was my mind as I thought that, or my mind the glass, and that was the reason for the fear and the cold and also for the sense of growing excitement and a fear then, a different kind of fear, that I would not be able to do anything with this excitement, that it would be my failure, my failure to realize what I now saw were the real possibilities of the glass, a failure for which I would never be able to forgive myself, though a part of me would always know or perhaps only believe that it was in the nature of my insight that there could be no realization of it, that it was precisely an insight about non-realization, but by then, wrote Harsnet, it had all become too complicated, too extreme, I did not want to know any of it until it was all over, until I had made my effort, perhaps it had been a mistake to come in and sit there with the glass through the night with the moon shining so brightly, it must have been full, or nearly full, unnaturally bright anyway, something to do with the solstice perhaps, to sit in the room with the glass alone or with the moon alone might have been bearable, in the dark with the glass or in the moonlight in an empty room, but the two together, the glass and the moon, that was perhaps the mistake. I had gone too far and experienced too much, I needed to slow down, to get back to the small things, the practical things, to measuring and cutting and fixing, and it was with relief that I noticed that daylight had begun to invade the room, I kept quite still, I held the glass firmly in my gaze, gradually the elements already worked on began to emerge, some more clearly than others, some in outline only and some only when they impeded the free flow of light through the glass, until the sun came up and was reflected back from the windows of the house opposite and I could sit and look at the glass and think back through the work and the mistakes and the few successes, and sense again with that sickening feeling in the pit of the stomach that the whole of the right hand side of the lower panel was still a mess, nothing there had been resolved, but then I drew back from that, though it kept trying to pull me back to itself, and concentrated on what was beginning to work, on the left hand areas both top and bottom and on the elegance of the frame and the joy of seeing the bare walls and the wainscoting appear through the empty areas, and as I moved round so different parts of the room appeared and the relation of the surface of the glass to what lay behind changed, precision and fluidity, precision and fluidity, he wrote, choice and chance, not choice alone and chance alone but the two together, that is why delay, not stoppage and not flow but delay, delay in glass, he wrote, as when the plane is late and you should have been gone, have already arrived perhaps, but you are still there, or the sprinter beats the gun and the whole field is called back, the race could have been over but it has not yet started. Now I Joseph was walking, and I walked not. And I looked up to the air and saw the air in amazement. And I looked up unto the pole of the heaven and saw it standing still, and the fowls of the heavens without motion. And I looked upon the earth and saw a dish set, and work-men lying by it, and their hands were in the dish: and they that were chewing chewed not, and they that were lifting the food lifted it not, and they that put it to their mouth put it not thereto, but the faces of all of them were looking

40

upward. And behold there were sheep being driven, and they went not forward but stood still; and the shepherd lifted his hand to smite them with his staff, and his hand remained up. And I looked upon the stream of the river and saw the mouths of the kids upon the water and they drank not. And of a sudden all things moved onward in their course. 1 cauliflower, 1 lb. carrots, 1 lb. onions, 1 celery, 1 pepper, shoelaces, library, memo pad, string, matches, toy-shop. The question that is never asked, wrote Harsnet (typed Goldberg), is the one that concerns the quality of life. What kind of life do you wish to lead? Is food and comfort the be-all and end-all? Why not if you no longer believe in God or even inspiration and genius? If there is only the mechanical operation of the spirit? Steam engines, he wrote. Every little cog plays its part. Every piston moves because every little cog plays its part. Eventually, it drives its load forward. But a work of art, so-called, is not a machine, he wrote. It can get nowhere, it can move nothing. From stimulation to ejaculation, he wrote. From ejaculation to insemination. But not in the so-called work of art. From the sea to the cloud, he wrote. From the cloud back to the land as rain. But not in the so-called work of art. Art is not a machine, he wrote, and it is not an organism. It is a pseudo-machine, a pseudo-organism. The Bride, he wrote. The Bachelors. The Pulley. The Cooler. The Moulds. The Scissors. The Grinder. The Gas. The Waterfall. The Mist. The Sieves. The Beginning of Exaltations and Beatifications, he wrote. Being an Effective Spirit in the Beautiful West, he wrote. Being in the Retinue of Osiris. Being Satisfied with the Food of Wenhofer. Delay as the function of art, he wrote. Nothing happens in this work, he wrote, but what of the world? Round and round. Up and down and up again. The last imitation, he wrote. How many have thought that though? That theirs would be the last, the true one, and after that there would be no need for more? Folly, he wrote. The folly of it. There is no last word, he wrote, and Goldberg, seizing his felt-tip pen, wrote in the margin *no last*. He licked the tip of the pen and added: *word*. Folly of last words as of first, wrote Harsnet. Always in the middle, he wrote. Never never never never never. Yet each to be written and spoken as though the last. Each picture painted *ditto*. And what's one more or less? Goldberg's face when I told him, he wrote. Where? he kept asking, where? I told him, Between junctions seventeen and eighteen. But why? he kept asking. Why? I didn't see the point, I said. You didn't what? he said. Fat already then, twenty-two, twenty-three, five eight but over fifteen stone. You didn't what? Face white, jaws shaking: You didn't what? It wasn't for you to see the point, he said. It was my painting. If that painting is lost, he said, I will never paint another, and you will be responsible. I am responsible, I said. That painting was mine, he said. And the other was mine, I said. I dumped them both. I don't give two farts for yours, he said, but you have just dumped mine on a motorway layby. My best picture, he said. The only one I ever felt got near to saying what I wanted to say. It might have won, I said, and you know what you think of prizes. You prick, he said, I should never have let you take them up. I trusted you, he said. What did you do it for, you – ? he said, bunching his right hand into a fist and pressing it in agony into his left palm. Are you crazy or something? I told you, I said to him, I suddenly didn't see any point in it. I suddenly agreed with you about prizes and fame and the rest. Suddenly. Just like that. There was no point in going on then. Where? he said. Show me where on the map. I don't know where on the map, I said. I told you, between junctions seventeen and eighteen. Going up? he said. Going up, I said. I should never have trusted you with it, he said. My best picture. You didn't want to win their lousy prize, did you? I said. You did too, he said. You must have. You put in for it. We both wanted to win, I said, and now we've been saved from temptation. He tried to hit me, kept pummelling me with his podgy fists, but he couldn't summon up the necessary enthusiasm. I'll have to get out and look for it, he said. I kept quiet. I'll phone the police, he said. Someone may have picked them up. Did you leave them there on the verge?

he asked me. I told you, I said to him, I just pulled in and heaved them out. Down a grassy slope. You shit, he said. You shit. It didn't stop me going on, but it stopped him. Your heart was never in it, I said to him later. You ruined my life, he said. One moment and my whole life was ruined. But later still he admitted he'd had his doubts. After his first TV series I said to him: Aren't you happier as a media critic, putting shitty artists in their places, than as a failed shitty artist being put in his place? Happier? he said, his blue eyes fixed on my face in that mad way he sometimes has. Do I look happier? he said. Yes, I said. More fulfilled. I had a feeling it would be for the best, I said, when I stopped on the hard shoulder that day. I didn't dump them straight away, you know, I said. Though I had made up my mind. I stopped the car and thought for a bit. Then I opened the back door and out they went. I will never forgive you as long as I live, he said. But he was laughing. Look me in the eye, I said. Look me in the eye Goldberg and tell me whether that picture was any good. What if it wasn't? he said. Winning the John Moores would have given me just the confidence I needed. I'd have got better. You'd have got better anyway, I told him. If you'd gone on. But you didn't. Goldberg, pushing the hair out of his eyes with his forearm, dragged the pad towards him and wrote: Appendix on the real facts? Or let him damn himself with his own words? In a hundred years' time, I said to him, wrote Harsnet (and Goldberg, putting the pad aside, began to type again), in a hundred years' time I said to him, (he typed) no one will remember either you or me. In ten years' time, I said to him, wrote Harsnet (typed Goldberg), they may still remember us both. But not in a hundred. That's not the point, he said. It wasn't your painting, it wasn't up to you to decide for me. It was in my car, I said. I just don't understand you, he said. I suddenly decided I didn't see any point in submitting them, I said. And they weren't worth transporting all the way back. I didn't feel comfortable with them in there with me, I said. Exuding hope. Exuding hope? he said, as if he didn't understand English any more. Well, there it is, I said. It's done now. But he took his car and drove all the way up. Must have stopped every ten yards between junctions seventeen and eighteen. Not a trace of them. It was raining by then anyway. Wouldn't speak to me for six months, but then his natural goodness of heart, as well perhaps as his gradual realization that I might have been right, that perhaps I had saved him from a fate worse than death, made it impossible for him to keep it up. When we met at the Bacon show and I smiled at him he smiled back at once, then remembered and tried to scowl, but couldn't and we both burst out laughing. I have put away my brushes for ever, he said. Meaningless words. It's not the stopping or the burning or the escaping to Africa that will make an end of it. It has to be there in the work. The end has to be built in. Otherwise as meaningless as any other gesture, as deeply rooted in the moment, in how one is feeling or what one has eaten or who one has been seeing. And in that case, wrote Harsnet, there is always the possibility that it will not be the end but a simple pause, a mere hiatus. Whereas I, wrote Harsnet, have become something of an expert on real endings, on true endings. The real end must be like counting one then two then three. No doubt about it. One is unique, two is double, three is infinity. No need to go on after three. One the glass, two the show, three the end. So Harsnet. And Goldberg, pushing the hair out of his eyes and wiping his face at the same time with his sleeve, pushed away the typewriter, pulled the pad towards him, seized the felt-tip pen, and wrote: He later admitted that he had merely said between seventeen and eighteen as a manner of speaking. He never looked at the exit numbers, he said later, but he was sure it was between two exits on the M6 to Liverpool, roughly between seventeen and eighteen. He later said – Goldberg pushed the pad aside and returned to his task of transcription. It becomes clear after one has been working at something for several weeks, he typed (as Harsnet had written), that one is not going to achieve what one had hoped for. The question is then, wrote Harsnet, whether to settle for less or start again. But again is always an illusion, wrote Harsnet, for it would also become clear, the second time round, after several weeks, that one was not doing what one had hoped to do. Despite the hard work. Despite the enthusiasm. Had one hoped for too much or has something gone wrong? he wrote. But why does it always go wrong? Tried soaking the matches in paint, he wrote, and firing from toy cannon. Three shots from three different positions. Had been dreaming about this for a long time, he wrote. The idea of the directed arbitrary. My search for the right kind of toy cannon. I knew what I wanted, but I couldn't find it. But eventually did. The excitement with which I brought it home. Set it up. I didn't go straight ahead with it. Wanted to savour the pleasure of what was to come. But in the end very disappointing. As is often the case, some last-minute idea blossoms while what had seemed a brilliant solution and been pondered for ages falls quite flat. That is why there has to be the big glass and the notes in the box, not the glass alone or the notes alone, but the box, with all my preliminary notes and measurements, all my plans and blueprints, and then the glass, with the end product of all those notes visible on its surface. Consider, he wrote. Where is the image? Where is the surface? What is the status of the image? Shadow of another reality? Not imitation of shadow. Not reproduction of shadow. But shadow itself. Always it is elsewhere, wrote Harsnet. But to us it comes as echo, shadow. Thus two dimensional representation of a three dimensional world, itself only the three dimensional representation of a four dimensional world. Perhaps. So: where is it happening? Not only a question about the big glass. Not only a question about art. The idea that it is happening elsewhere prevalent in our lives. Is it an illusion to imagine that this is a merely modern phenomenon? he wrote. That other ages did not feel this too? Is it not perhaps inevitable for all creatures with imagination, all creatures which can say no? Religions purvey illusion that with enough effort and humility you can get to that elsewhere. Perhaps only in the next life. But you can get there. Yet our art persists in trying to render

45

the world as though it were here, now, available, he wrote. As though there were no elsewhere and no need of an elsewhere. All mesmerized by this folly, he wrote, all the Goldbergs and McGrindles, the Mosses and Baiocchis, the Honeymen and McGoughs. Sumptuous richness of the textures. The way the drapery falls. How he is in love with flesh and conveys that love to us. Bah! So Harsnet. And Goldberg, in his pad: I have never said or written any of the sentiments attributed to me here, though I have heard them from the mouths and read them from the pens of others. It is typical of painters, he wrote, to make these wild accusations, wild generalizations. If he only. It is canvas and paint, wrote Harsnet, and Goldberg settled himself to type on. It is canvas and paint, he typed, and that is all. But, wrote Harsnet (typed Goldberg), that is no big deal either, as the Americans seem to think. Why want to celebrate the act of applying paint to canvas? I can think of nothing more disgusting or unpleasant, he wrote. Certainly of few things more uninteresting. Matched only perhaps by the uninterestingness of the minds and souls of such painters. Art in America synonymous with success, he wrote, and telling the truth reduced to baring the breast. The smallness of it, he wrote. The dreariness of it. And taken seriously not only there but here as well, by critics who themselves long for success, and long too to lay bare their own poor breasts. So Harsnet. The reason why I have a soft spot for this notebook, he wrote. In this notebook, recording my random thoughts day after day as I work on the big glass, I can keep my distance from the big glass. I report on its progress (or lack of it), that is all. I mutter to myself (or curse), that is all. Today, such and such. Moved forward in this way. Fell back in that way. No more. As when asked to fill in questionnaire and give details of age, sex, height, colour hair, etc. That is all. But the point is there can never be any more. That is what Kafka understood. What is *Metamorphosis* except progress report on the disintegration of a body? Kafka turns the secret weapon of the novel against itself. What do I mean by that? he wrote. I mean that the

46

novel has always given the impression that third person narration can narrate what it is I am feeling. (Or first person narration for that matter.) What Kafka discovers is that there is no direct relation between what I feel and what happens to me. All of Kafka nothing but report to the Academy, presented by a scrupulous and conscientious clerk. Kafka's genius lies in his having grasped that this was much more true to experience, much more realistic, than the rich sensuality and feeling for the individual etc. etc. of Lawrence and his much more pathetic followers. Don't tell, show – the slogan that keeps this myth from exploding. The slogan of blinkered professors and dull art critics, who, as always, are a couple of hundred years out of date. So Harsnet. And Goldberg, on his pad: If the fool had ever bothered to read what I have written on the subject in the essay on aura and the hour he would not have flailed about as he does here. Typical of artists to read nothing except what they happen upon and then to pontificate about life and art and the way the world is going. He talks of responsibility, wrote Goldberg, half-tearing the page of his pad in his hurry to turn it over without breaking the flow of his thought, but where is his own sense of it? My son, he wrote, moving on to a new page, my son, who is a keen footballer and a passionate supporter of our local team, Brighton and Hove Albion (the Seagulls), was surprised the other day when, looking in on one of the team's training sessions in the sports pavilion of the University of Sussex, he. Pushing aside the pad he returned to his task. Where does an artist like Kafka come from? he typed, squinting at his erstwhile friend's crumpled manuscript. Where are the rules that can legislate for someone like that? he typed (as Harsnet had written). Genius is precisely the word one does not feel tempted to use. Genius is Michelangelo at work on the Sistine ceiling. Genius is Wordsworth peering down from Snowdon in the mist. Genius is the bust of Beethoven and Keats dying and Shelley dying and the size of *War and Peace* and poor old Sartre banging away at his trilogy and Hemingway paring it down to its essence and Monet unable to distinguish colours any more and Picasso staring out at the camera with his chest bare and his eyes blazing and Cézanne snarling like a dog and then walking out of Aix with his canvas and paints on his back to paint that mountain and Byron dying and Pushkin dying and all the rest of it. That is Genius, wrote Harsnet. But no more interesting was my *Picture Painted by a Genius* of 1954, no more interesting my *Replica of a Diploma Submitted in Lieu of an Original Composition for the Award of a Degree*. How to avoid the traps of both Genius and Whimsy? wrote Harsnet (typed Goldberg). How to move between pretentiousness and cynicism? There are two things fatal to the the development of any artist, Leiris said, one is success and the other is failure. But he could equally well have said one is enthusiasm and the other is cynicism, one is facility and the other is aridity, one is gregariousness and the other is solitude, one is the belief that no one has ever done anything of value before and the other is the belief that everything has already been done, one is spontaneity and the other is cerebration, one is joy and the other is despair, one is heart and the other is mind, one is the garret and the other is the penthouse, one is sincerity and the other is irony, one is Jung and the other is Freud, one is Rimbaud and the other is Mallarmé, one is wine and the other is coffee, one is rags and the other is riches, one is women and the other is celibacy, one is health and the other is disease, one is meat and the other is vegetables, one is life and the other is death, one is everything in upper case and the other is everything in lower case, one is everything in roman and the other is everything in italics. So Harsnet. Fatal, he wrote (and Goldberg typed). Both are fatal. Tried using popgun after fiasco of toy cannon, he wrote, but that was too violent where other was too weak. Trouble too on lower panel, right hand side, he wrote. Waterfall clutters too much. Need something different but don't know what. Still hankering after round peep-hole but still afraid of damaging glass. Waterfall or ladder, he wrote. Steps leading from lower to higher, from higher to lower. Ladder without rungs? he wrote. Inverted waterfall? (No Newton here.)

The point about the big glass, he wrote, is that there is no right way up and so there is no upside down. Yet panels have to be one above the other, not side by side. Elements in top panel floating in space. In lower panel vanishing point clear and perspective of each element rigorous. But our sense of its space will always depend on where it is placed. Put against open window giving onto garden full of trees and it is one thing. Place in gallery with no windows and visitors everywhere looking at pictures on walls and it is something else. Place high up against open sky and moving clouds and it is something else again. By introduction of glass, he wrote, relation of background to foreground radically altered. Avoid the retinal, he wrote, but not the image. Image-concept, concept-image, he wrote. Glass/box//box/glass, he wrote. Retain perspective but remove notion of window, he wrote. In top panel no perspective, shadow only, milky way, he wrote. Fist and mystery, he wrote. Fist strikes and time condenses: mystery glows and time dilates. My ideal, he wrote, fist and mystery, both. When I glimpse such a combination my heart beats faster. That is all there is to it. In *Les Noces* and *Symphony of Psalms*. In *Dans le labyrinthe* and 'Boy of Winander'. In Bonnard's *Window* and Breughel's *Children's Games*. All my life a preparation for my version of this combination? he wrote. See it in place, he wrote. Never mind where so long as it is a public space. Not this room. See it installed in a public place and then bow out. Not finished till installed, he wrote. So long as it remains in this room, he wrote, it is not finished. Yet in a public place it will not take up any space. It will not elbow anything else out of the way. 'My space on this wall, get off' – the curse of the gallery system, of the collecting syndrome. Instead, my glass will be a lens to see the rest through. A means of making the visitor delay. Not look at but look with. It all comes back, wrote Harsnet (typed Goldberg), to the Kafka phenomenon. I understood this the first time I read him, he wrote, in that smelly room in Hackney. I could not formulate it to myself then but I felt the uniqueness. Because nothing in his work stands up and

49

says: Look at me, look how true, beautiful, profound, etc. *Speculum humanae salvationis*, he wrote. *Speculum mundi.* The glass of the salvation of humanity, he wrote. The glass of the world. Not glass to reflect a bit of the world, but a crystal ball to look into so as to understand the world. The big glass, he wrote. Monstrous in this small room, though in the light of the day it reverts to its ordinary size, two biggish panels of glass, steel frame and stand, 227.5 x 175.8 cm. (109¼ x 69¼ inches). Perhaps a way should be found of ensuring that we experience both the ordinariness and the extraordinariness of the glass, he wrote. In a gallery all by itself? But then I lose what I most want from it, that it be in a room with other objects. So perhaps it will have to fend for itself. Its purity will protect it. At a certain point, he wrote, you have to let go, he wrote, you have to let it go. That is what the third part of the project means. Diana unleashing the hounds, he wrote. Thought yesterday of including hounds in some form or other: Melampus, Ichnobates, Pamphagus, Dorceus, Oribasos, Nobrophonos, Theron, Laelaps, Prerelas, Agre. The principle I have to stick to, wrote Harsnet (typed Goldberg) is that of the rebus: a boat, a house, a letter, a word. Mistake of the old type of interpretation was to fit all into a single story, a single world. But they come from different worlds. The river from the world of rivers. The house from the world of houses. The letter from the world of letters. And so on. And as they only exist, these many worlds, in dreams, so they only exist in a work of art. The old painters knew this. Lost with tedious Florentine allegorising. Genius of Picasso to recall us to this, with his combinations of life-class drawing, cubism, collage, lettering, etc. Escape from 500 years of the tyranny of the eye, the brain. The I. Yet do not underestimate the pain of letting go, he wrote. Do not underestimate the cost. Pain and joy both, he wrote. Those Picasso collages of 1910-14 the ancestors of my delays, he wrote. The ego will brook no delay, he wrote. Capitalism will brook no delay. It is up to us to institute delay, he wrote. In the big glass, he wrote, many stories, many half stories, many

50

fragments. The story of the scissors. Of the grinder. Of the sieves. Of the policeman and the judge. Of the bride. Of the bachelors. Of Diana. Of the 4D world. Yet all must be precise, he wrote. Self-sufficient. Yet infinitely expandable. Grand aims, he wrote, but no grand gestures. Only that which is precise has resonance, he wrote. Vermeer, not Delacroix. Morandi, not Rothko. Leave such comparisons to others, he wrote. Leave to Goldberg and Pizzetti, Moss and McGrindle. And Goldberg in his pad: N.B. his almost pathological need to denigrate critics and criticism. The image of the critic as scape-goat in post-Romantic art, wrote Goldberg. Keats. Wordsworth at Cambridge. Proust and Sainte-Beuve. Monet. Cézanne. Schoenberg. Stravinsky. Develop, he wrote. He pushed the pad aside and returned to his typing. Letter from Marcus, he typed (as Harsnet had written). Invitation for w/e. Accept? Work on big glass slowing down, wrote Harsnet. Not to say drying up completely. After all these months of forward movement only to be expected. Or so I keep telling myself. But do I believe it? Mistake though to make fetish of work, he wrote. It all depends on the intensity of the work, not the amount. But do I believe that? In recent days, he wrote, perhaps because Spring is upon us, I have been putting in the hours but the intensity has gone. Danger of harming the work. Danger of doing something irrevocable and wrong because initial impetus lost and clue that will lead me to the centre not yet found. As always, middle game greatest nightmare, he wrote. In my early work, he wrote, I in a sense dispensed with middles. The opening carried me forward straight to the end. Or, with the readymades, beginnings and ends were actually one. Perhaps in art today there is no longer a place for middles, he wrote. Middles were all right for Veronese, but today they no longer have a role. With the first stroke I have already reached the end, said Picasso. I grow bored with the sheer size of the glass and have to force myself to continue, he wrote. And yet, he wrote, if the glass is to be any sort of advance, it will be because of the middle. Because it is nothing but a middle, without beginning or end. The

51

beauty of glass, he wrote, is this, that the surface does not have to be covered. Much of the middle, in fact, he wrote, will depend on where it is set up. If I could only resolve that lower right hand panel though, he wrote, or even decide once and for all to leave it empty, then perhaps the boredom would disappear. Boredom a sign of failure, he wrote. If I am bored then I have not found the way to do what I wanted to do. Bored with the assertion of the central place of boredom in human affairs, he wrote. Leave that to Warhol, etc. American denial of the human spirit, he wrote. Already predicted by Toqueville. Natural end of journey begun by Pilgrim Fathers is Warhol's Marilyn, he wrote. Had they but known. The real question, he wrote, is how to keep hold of a richer view of the possibilities of life while denying the consolations of an afterlife, denying the special destiny of man, denying the Value of Civilization (Nietzsche). Danny, he wrote. Queen's gambit. Terrible trouble after bad exchange. Position not unlike Morphy-Schrufer, Paris, 1859, before Morphy's knight move on B5. Lost thread and lucky to draw. But game did nothing for the glass, as I had hoped. Block still there. Delay, he wrote. Neither flowing with time (materialism), nor denying time (romanticism). A time for disinterested contemplation, he wrote. Not just a delay in glass, he wrote, but glass as mirror of delay. *Glass*, wrote Goldberg in the margin, *mirror of delay*. Mirror of delay and means of delay, wrote Harsnet (and Goldberg typed). Not the bottle that guarantees to turn your grey hair black or make your bald pate sprout again, but something else. A hiatus in nature. As in *Protevangelium*: And I looked up into the pole of the heavens and saw it standing still, and the fowls of the heavens without motion... And of a sudden all things moved onward in their course. Every image, of its nature, he wrote, freezes the world. For centuries we have tried to pretend that this was not the case. We cannot, with the coming of moving film, go on with this pretence. So what can we do? What must we do? One solution to paint those moments when world *is* frozen, when we experience time as standing still: when we look in mirrors, or on hot afternoons. Bonnard painted hot afternoons in mirrors. Magritte did it by playing with paradox: day and night both; picture and landscape both. Moving at best, but too often tricksy. How though to get sense of whole world pausing, before moving on? Impossible if you think of painting as image of piece of world. But if you think of it as model of whole world, as great cathedrals were said to be, or physicists' models today? Marcus, wrote Harsnet (typed Goldberg). That exquisite house, not another in sight. Complaining about losing his sight. Black glasses even indoors. Tony more subdued than I'd remembered him. At 6 a.m. Marcus leaps out of bed and starts to play Victorian hymns on the little portable organ he has in his bedroom. Whole house starts to echo with the booming sound. Impossible to sleep. He comes to the end of one and without pause is off on another. Sometimes plays straight, sometimes starts to distort, hardly perceptible at first, then more and more, until he is producing wild expressionist shrieks or light medieval dances, then gradually the hymn reasserts itself until all is as it should be. Then all of a sudden, silence. You keep waiting for more but it doesn't come. He works till lunch, then wanders into the kitchen and has long argument with Tony, or perhaps a discussion about the best way to cook trout or whether or not to sack the gardener. In the afternoon he starts by sleeping, then takes over the kitchen and insists on preparing extravagant five-course meals. Had me take him into Salisbury to the oculist. Pretends he can't go anywhere alone and this is a chance for Tony to get some time to himself. Swore like a trooper under his breath as the bus swayed through the leafy lanes, saying he could no longer make out the landmarks, that he knew such and such a tree or house was in such and such a place, he'd passed it so often in the bus, but now could barely see it. New little clavichord in his study, seventeenth century, and over his desk his charts and diagrams. Photo of Schoenberg and Gershwin playing tennis, and reproduction of Dürer's *Melancholia*. Phenomenal energy still. After cooking supper that was more like a banquet than an ordinary meal he played us some medieval things on the organ and then some Elizabethan things on the clavichord. Left him still playing at midnight and collapsed into bed. Eerie silence of the countryside. Will never get used to it. And then, just after I'd fallen asleep, as I thought, there was the damned organ moaning away and it was 6 a.m. again. Tony in the kitchen. Death of his father. Long string of jokes about the funeral, as though to show how well he was taking it. Painful. At the door, one more joke, rather good. Perelman's publishers sent Groucho Marx a copy of P's first book soliciting a puff. 'From the moment I picked up this book to the moment I put it down,' wrote GM, 'I couldn't stop laughing. One of these days I intend to read it.' As I left I asked Marcus to remove his dark glasses so I could look at his face. He refused, said the light hurt his eyes. Memory of him standing there waving with two black holes in the middle of his face. Wouldn't leave me all through the following night as I worked on the glass. And those beautiful expressive hands of his flying over the keyboard of the little painted organ. Sense of excessive energy, no outlet, as though he's going to burst into a million pieces if some inner pressure doesn't abate. He wanted to play at the funeral but Tony's mother wouldn't let him. Cursed the American planes. Said they would force him to move again. One fighter flying low overhead can ruin a whole day's work. In the middle of working on a difficult piece I can almost feel my ears grow, he said. I start to hear everything much better than I normally do. I hear the grass grow, for instance. Look at Schoenberg's ears, he said. Look at Stravinsky's. Those aren't ears, he said, those are receiving dishes. But why this passion for hearing more, seeing more, experiencing more? Why not stay with what we normally hear and see and feel? Because it's not grand enough? Not important enough? The desire for transfiguration, wrote Harsnet. The desire for resurrection in this life. The desire for a world freed of banality, confusion. Why not the triumph of the ordinary? he wrote. The transfiguration of the contingent? That Christian ache for redemption, he wrote. I know it well. I know

54

from where it comes and where it wishes to get to. But redemption from what? Even denial à la Warhol, cynicism à la Warhol nothing but inverted nostalgia for a lost transcendental. As if it had ever been there. All haunted by the sense of a sacred space, a sacred time. Which the big glass will not only deny but show up for what it is: narcissism, regression, the refusal to see things as they are. (The Death of Images.) Set up glass in centre of gallery, he wrote. Not an object to be looked at and admired. Not elbowing others out of the way. It is and is not there. It delays your approach to Klee, Picasso, Bacon, Pollock. That is all. A slight delay as you skirt round it. A barely perceptible delay as you gaze through it. Why this need to imagine it finished, installed, looked at by other eyes? he wrote. Is it because I am at a loss as to how to go on? No, he wrote. My sense of how to go on determined by the vividness of my imagination of what it will be like when done. A struggle to realize what in some sense already exists. Strong sense of an object, he wrote, not an image. Incorporate Marcus' black glasses? he wrote. Yesterday set up conditions for Milky Way, he wrote. Gauze over radiator photographed three times as currents moved it. Sense suddenly of peace. No hurry. Glass guiding me where I must be going. But trouble with Bride, he wrote. Oxidization. Need to find other method of putting her on. Nevertheless, he wrote (and Goldberg typed), it is proceeding according to plan. Leading me where I have always wanted to go yet never known how. Understood that after w/e in Wiltshire. Going away as a means of discovering what was really happening here, he wrote. No need to detail now. Only to say I came back and saw glass as another might see it. After eight months' work it has acquired a life of its own. A personality of its own. Though in one sense only just begun. After all the doubts and uncertainties, wrote Harsnet, most of which I did not admit to myself, or else tried to pretend were an integral part of the project, sense now that it is on its way. Even bottom right may be all right as it is. Key to everything the idea of the glass. And then the idea (how did it come to me?) that it must not simply be glass but big glass. After that only a matter of confidence. Of holding on. The plans in place. Strategy and tactics all there in the box. Yet doubts remain. Till realized difficult to know if idea is really valid. Will really yield what I want it to. You can dream and dream but only what happens in this room night after night is important. The solution of each individual problem. The solution of the problem of relating the individual solutions to each other. Or refusing to relate them. So much bigger than anything I have ever undertaken, he wrote. The initial terror. Terror and excitement. In the heart. In the stomach. That is the mystery, he wrote. To keep it from flowing away from you and yet to keep it going. To place one item, one element, in relation to all the others, and yet to keep space open for further elements. Time does not exist in the big glass, he wrote. Only exposure will provide it. Exposure to viewer. If only there was a way for each viewer to leave his mark. Each eye that looks to wear away the glass a little bit. My dream of a book whose print fades a little each time it is read until the pages are blank. Perhaps provide each viewer with specially prepared spectacles? Hang those on big glass? Too fussy. Find another solution, wrote Harsnet. Find way of treating glass so as to respond to viewer's gaze? Can that be done? Not to be true to the materials but false to them! he wrote. Find a way of allowing each viewer to make his own impact on the glass, he wrote, to indicate that viewing is not a neutral activity. Remove passivity from the process of viewing, he wrote. Bring time back into the work, he wrote. The time of viewing as well as the time of making. And yet the glass itself is about the emptiness of time, he wrote. Time is not full, he wrote. It is not alive with meaning. A only relates to B because I have put them there. It is important, he wrote, to show that there is no natural link between them. The fatal delay, he wrote, and Goldberg, seizing his pen, scribbled in the margin: *fatal delay*. The Bride, wrote Harsnet (and Goldberg went on typing), fails to get impregnated. The Bachelors, he wrote, fail to achieve their desire. The distance between them, he wrote, is not so much great as unbridgeable. Sex in the head, he wrote. Each remains in his or her half, dreaming of the other. Out of that what can come? Nothing can come of nothing, he wrote. That is why the glass is dedicated to Diana. Why it is the colour of the moon and made in the light of the moon. It all boils down, wrote Harsnet (typed Goldberg), to the question of true causality. Children begotten by arbitrary spasm, he wrote. Ditto artworks. Lack of relation, he wrote, between input and output. The choice is to ignore this or to draw attention to it. I cannot ignore it. So I have chosen to make an image of the failure of cause to relate to effect. Delay in glass is delay in life, he wrote. Fatal delay, he wrote. Between A and B falls the shadow, he wrote. If the Bachelors could impregnate the Bride, he wrote, then art would flourish. Then I would be an artisan, quietly learning my trade at the feet of a master and passing it on in turn to my apprentices. But that is not how it is, he wrote. There is no meaning in the world, so there is no meaning in art. To go on acting as though there were is to add to the layers of falsehood which already cover our (so-called) civilization. What needs to be done, he wrote, is to strip away, not to add. Yet all art is addition. Even when it speaks of stripping it still adds. How then to escape the falsity? he wrote. The death of images, he wrote. My catalogue essay to end all catalogue essays. I copy it down here to help me go forward. It was in those far-off days as they strolled through the parks and boulevards of the great cities of the West, that people first began to speak of the death of images. Soon it had become one of the main topics of conversation. It was discussed with passion and anxiety in small groups and in large assemblies, in salons and cafés, in bars and in clubs. Friends talked the matter over far into the night and then went home, to their families or to the loneliness of dingy bed-sitting rooms, to carry on the debate in diaries and notebooks, poems and letters. No one knew what had first led to the rumour that soon images would die, nor how the rumour had grown into conviction and conviction into certainty. One young man, unable to tolerate the thought, burned himself alive in a public square. A girl of twelve turned her face to the wall, refused all nourishment, and so passed away. Others, more robust or less perceptive, found, on the contrary, a renewed zest for life in the perpetual animated discussions occasioned by the topic. A distinguished philosopher, much admired in the profession, became a celebrity overnight when he wrote in a Sunday paper that what all the varied responses had in common was the forlorn belief that somehow, through talk or action, the decisive event would be warded off. But, he pointed out, no one could possibly conceive what life would be like after the death of images. Without images, he said, there would not even be the wherewithal to talk about the death of images. Language itself, he said, would cease to function as it had always functioned, it would only be a strange dead thing, smouldering perhaps, but burnt out, no longer conveying any meaning. That, he said, was, strictly speaking, inconceivable. So long as we have language, he argued, we simply cannot conceive it. And without language we would not be able to conceive it either. But may it not be the case, he suggested, that images have already died and we are not aware of it? You who read me, he concluded, you who think you understand me, must try to imagine what it would be like not to understand me. To read me and think you understand me and yet not to understand me. Only if you do that will you be able to say with confidence that I am wrong, that what I am suggesting has not yet come to pass, that there is still time. His words were taken up by many who would not have dreamed of opening any of his more technical works, and he came to be in great demand as a speaker at rallies and at the numerous conferences and seminars on the death of images organized by the Universities, the Churches and the innumerable Humanist organizations which had mushroomed in the immediately preceding decades. Even those who had never heard of him mouthed his words, repeating them to others as though they had just thought of them themselves, which perhaps they had, for there is surely such a thing as a spirit of the times. But it did not bring an end to the speculation and confusion which was rending the civilized world. As a leading writer put it, after casting doubts on the appropriateness of the philosopher's imagery, just because his answer was probably the right one it was in effect no answer at all. The summer, which was a glorious one that year, gave way to a gusty autumn, and, as is the way with these things, after the autumn came the winter. That was the year when, in the parks and boulevards of the great cities of the West, people first began to talk about the death of images. So Harsnet. And Goldberg, seizing his pen, scribbled in the margin: *Death of images – see cat. Dusseldorf exhib. 8.10.62.* Hegel, wrote Harsnet (and Goldberg typed). Hölderlin. Wittgenstein. Kafka. That is why producing yet more images, he wrote, is like eating cardboard. Nightmare, he wrote. Found myself out in the snow but the snow had turned into cotton wool. World gradually being covered in cotton wool. Not cold, so at first quite pleasant. Then sudden realization that it would not stop. That it would never stop. That it would gradually cover the earth, the trees, me. Escape impossible. Breathing it in through the nose, the mouth. Sense of not unpleasant suffocation. My horror at the fact that it was not unpleasant, that I was almost enjoying it, and that it was killing me. That is what words are today, he wrote. What images are. Two monstrosities, wrote Borges, mirrors and procreation, for both duplicate existence. In contrast, wrote Harsnet (typed Goldberg), the big glass. Set it up against the window, he wrote. Or on terrace. A mere delay in seeing the world. Even in gallery, he wrote, it will disturb no one, merely make it a little more difficult to get from one side of the room to the other. Why this urge to add, constantly to add? he wrote. Pictures, he wrote, statues, books, children. Goldberg and his brood, he wrote. Rosenblum that day in the queue at Camisi's: What did the good Lord create us for if not to be fathers? And McGrindle, very matter of fact though drunk as usual: I have sixteen children, seven by my first marriage, four by my second, my second wife had two of her own, that makes thirteen, and three from my third, sixteen, and I am proud to say I have been able to give them all a good education and every chance in life without ever compromising my integrity. As if every sentence he had ever written had not cried out to the heavens that the man had as much integrity as a rotten tree-trunk. Goldberg taking out his polka-dotted handkerchief and wiping his brow, his cheeks, his neck, pushed aside the typewriter and seized his pen. Dragging the pad towards him he found a clean page and wrote: Dear Harsnet, I know you never answer my letters or return my calls, and I know that you handed over your notes to me on the understanding that I could do what I liked with them and not bother you, but I have to say that while there is much in them that I admire, as I will always admire much in you, no matter what, there is also much in them that seems to me to be puerile and, to put it mildly, bigoted. I have decided, however, in the interests of posterity, to cut nothing, though I may take the liberty of annotating the text here and there, putting some of the facts straight and referring the reader to related documents, such as interviews you once gave or books and articles on you which have since appeared. I know none of this interests you any longer, he wrote, and that you hold yourself, or pretend to hold yourself, aloof from the world, and in particular from the world of art. You are, or pretend to be, indifferent to whatever may happen to your reputation. Nevertheless I feel that I have a responsibility to the public and to the world of art both to present your unpublished writings in as comprehensible a form as possible, and at the same time to correct some of the misleading impressions these might give, not of course about yourself, but about others, casually mentioned here and there in the course of your jottings. I am not talking primarily about myself, he wrote, for it will be obvious to anyone who reads these notes that you have used me simply as a stalking horse for some of your more outrageous views and. Dear Harsnet, he wrote, tearing the sheet in his hurry to turn over the page, I know you never reply to letters and refuse to answer the door or the phone. I respect your privacy. Who would not? However, it seems to me that there is something a little perverse in leaving me your notes on the making of the Big Glass when you must have known perfectly well that they contained material I would be certain to find offensive. This is the main reason why I have not until recently felt able to face the task of transcribing them and editing them in the way they. Dear Harsnet, he wrote, I am not sure if this will reach you and I know that even if it does you will not reply. After all, since our last meeting, if one can call it a meeting, at the entrance to the sweet little National Gallery of Modern Art in Edinburgh, all those years ago, you have cut yourself off from your friends and well-wishers. I do not. Dear Harsnet, he wrote, I want simply to tell you that work on your notes connected with the Big Glass is at last under way and that I have remained scholarly and impartial throughout what has not been an easy task, in view of what you say about me and especially about my family, and which you must have known would give offense. However. Dear Harsnet, he wrote, just a brief note to let you know that work on the MSS you left with me is proceeding apace (at long last!) and will soon be ready for publication. I cannot express what a privilege it has been transcribing it and entering your very mind and spirit in the throes of creativity, as it were. Perhaps we can meet and talk about it all one of these days. Dear Harsnet, he wrote, my son, who is a keen supporter of Brighton and Hove Albion Association Football Club (The Seagulls), and who frequently goes to the sports centre of the University of Sussex to watch his team at their indoor training, was surprised the other day to see two figures distinctly older than the rest of the players. One of them, it was pointed out to him, was the great ex-Soviet chess player, Korchnoi, who is apparently training with the team in order to reach maximum physical fitness for his world title challenge to his arch-rival, the darling of the Soviets, Karpov. Imagine his surprise then, when, looking more closely, he identified the other man as. Dear Harsnet, he wrote, this is a message from the past. I just want to tell you. Goldberg, pushing

61

aside pad and pen, drew the little typewriter towards him and began to type again. The procreative metaphor, he typed (as Harsnet had written), has been the bane of art. It is not enough, wrote Harsnet, to deny that one conceives a work of art and brings it forth as a child is conceived and brought forth into the world. Human artefacts are not children, he wrote. They are made, not born. The colossal error of nineteenth-century anthropologists like Tyler was to imagine that there was no difference. The reaction to this of Saussure, Lévi-Strauss and their followers part and parcel of the modernist reaction to nineteenth-century art and culture. But the metaphor goes on haunting us, he wrote. Merely to deny it, even to prove its falsity, is not enough. The organic metaphor is so deeply rooted, he wrote, that ordinary refutation is not enough. In order to get rid of the whole web of interlinked concepts, myths, wishes and desires, one has to mine it from within. The sterility of the Bride, he wrote. The sterility of the Bachelors. Bride means nothing without Maid or Virgin, he wrote. Bachelor means nothing without Husband or Father. World of culture, not nature, he wrote. But a culture which is frozen, locked into its contradictions. The grinder, he wrote. The chariot and its onanistic litany, he wrote. It is emancipated horizontally, he wrote. Like the rest of the glass, he wrote, it defies the second law of thermo-dynamics. Why? Because in the imagination there is no friction. By the same token, he wrote, in the imagination there cannot be movement. Everything remains hypothetical. That is what happens in the big glass too, he wrote. But are things any different inside our culture? A sterile culture because a purely hypothetical one, he wrote. No reality, he wrote, only images masquerading as reality, only dreams masquerading as the real world. Is it only our culture? he wrote. TV and all that? Or endemic to all? All those lonely brides today, he wrote. All those lonely bachelors. The Grinder grinds but no chocolate emerges, he wrote. Glider, he wrote, Mallic Moulds, Scissors, Sieves. The circulation of the gas, he wrote. But it is only in the imagination of the Bride, of the Bachelors, of

62

the viewer. It cannot make the machine work. It can only generate anxiety, despair. The Bride strips herself, glowing with pleasure at seeing herself seen, but it is a poor solitary exercise, for she is only impregnated by her imagination. Hilda, he wrote, when I ventured to tell her all her troubles were her own fault: You are so cold. As though heat were an unquestioned good. You smile and remain unmoved, she said, just like father. And the others: You have such warmth! So much to give! If only you would let yourself go! Go where? Go where? wrote Harsnet (typed Goldberg). Where did they want me to go? Mushrooms grow in the dark, I said to Hilda. What's that to do with it? she said. Things grow in the warm darkness, I said, but I prefer it cold and moonlit. Romantic claptrap, she said. You think of yourself as a realist but you're really full of this romantic bullshit about the moon. Cold is bad, I said to her. Romantic is bad. Warmth is good. Realism is good. Now I know, I said to her. I will endeavour to act on this information. Is that all you can say? she said. Like Madge: Is that all you can say? Hitting me with her little fists, but I couldn't get the smile off my face. For some reason I couldn't, though I could see it was that which infuriated her more than anything. I wanted to but I couldn't. Your smile destroyed her, Goldberg said. She told me it was your smile that did it. Am I responsible for that? I asked him. Yes, he said. She was a wonderful girl and your smile destroyed her. You could have talked to her, he said, you could have explained. What was there to explain? I said. Anyway, she was the one who did the talking. You put up this front to protect yourself. There's really no need to be afraid. Which of them said that? Annie? No. I remember the words but not the face. Like the other day. Buying the wire. Hullo, how are you? What brings you to this part of town? I knew the face and knew at once that we had been intimate, but I had no idea who she was. Absolutely no idea. Is that a sign of age? Indifference? Or what? When I cannot even remember the names of the women I slept with? Or anything about them. Only the vague sensation that I had, once. Or had I? Almost as though it had all happened in another life. The embarrassment of not remembering. Good after that to return to the big glass. Good to lock the door and settle down with it. My *prisonnière*. The wire immediately resolved the problem of definition. Nice echo too of medieval stained glass, while helping to establish principle of making the utterly new out of the old, the ordinary, the commonplace – what could be more ordinary than fuse-wire? My old dream of a work which celebrates the contents of a pocket. Everything a pocket has ever carried in its time. Has cradled and protected. Has smothered and covered in dust: the sweets of childhood, the matches of adolescence, the pills of maturity. And all the rest of it. My attempt at an inventory of the entire contents of a jacket pocket for 1959. The surprises when I actually checked. The amazing number of sheer things. Mum furious that day when, aged seven, I emptied out the contents of her bag and arranged them on the table in descending order of size. The selectivity of archaeology what makes it so uninteresting. Then to turn the contents of a pocket into a work of art. Framed. Up there. Selectivity of course. How else? But selectivity so planned as to celebrate randomness. Impersonal rules, such as size, colour, alphabet, only to keep the mind from ordering in more banal ways. The old problem: How to give satisfying form without denying abundance, formlessness? Wire to define contours. Stick with mastic varnish, then seal with layer of lead foil pressed into wet paint and seal again with lead. Cover with second panel of glass, so that contents fully visible but inaccessible. Everything crystal clear but refusing to make sense. The more you try to decipher the more confusing it becomes. The whole problem of optimum distance, he wrote. Optimun distance of the spectator. My concern over this for almost as long as I can remember. Then the solution imposed by the glass. All problems resolved in one go because now for the first time question of optimum distance becomes an issue for the viewer. How the glass seems to be bringing together so many of my old themes, he wrote. Without my even being aware of it. That which is hidden is that which

64

is shown. The mystery of tattoos. Inventories. Time. And Goldberg in the margin: *Compendium of old themes*. As though in every life, wrote Harsnet (and Goldberg returned to his typing), if enough work has been done, enough determination shown, there is one final large summary, and that should be enough. Perhaps that is the difference, wrote Harsnet, between me and someone like Goldberg, for all his energy and ambition. He floats with the tide. There can be no summation for him because there is nothing there to sum up. The glass, he wrote, challenges the tide. It interposes a delay. Though in the long term, as I have said before, he wrote, it makes little difference, the tide always wins out, sooner or later all vanishes into the sea. Ignore the long term though, he wrote. Ignore deliberately. Start from where you are. Start from what you've got. Do not look up. Do not look back. One step and then another and then another and then another after that. Get rid of what you don't need, he wrote. Make do with the absolute minimum. Find the logic of each project. It cannot be known beforehand, he wrote. Each discovery is bought at a cost, he wrote. This is what the Goldbergs and McGrindles cannot understand. Not A *and* B but A *or* B. Eliminate the soggy, he wrote. Eliminate nostalgia. No solution because no problem, he wrote. Sleep, wake, cook, eat, go in, switch on light, examine prisoner, get down to work, finish work, write up notebook, sleep, wake, cook, eat. *La Tartine d'Albertine?* he wrote. Child's toy – my old dream. Each day a little advance, each day the surprising discovery. So Harsnet. And Goldberg, in his pad: Dear Harsnet, it may surprise you to hear that after all these years I am finally at work transcribing the notes you entrusted to me so many years ago, with a view to eventually publishing them. You may have thought I had thrown them away, or merely forgotten about them, and I was entitled to do either, since you explicitly said I was to do exactly what I liked with them, that you washed your hands of them completely. Or you may not have thought at all. Since you are so unwilling to communicate with your old friends they can only guess.

The fact is I did take it out once or twice, determined to do something with it, but other things, like earning enough to keep a roof over our heads and send the children to decent schools, always seemed to intervene. Do not think, he wrote, biting his lips in concentration, bending low over the page, blinking to keep the sweat out of his eyes, do not think that it was ever far from my mind. In fact, he wrote, I suspect that I will produce a better edition, one more worthy of its subject, now I have had time to mull over its implications and to watch the blossoming of your reputation. Do not think, he wrote, then pushed the pad aside, emptied his glass of orange juice and drew the typewriter to him. The tart, he typed (as Harsnet had written). Prisoner of conscience, he typed. La merde, la merde, toujours recommencée (what a recompense après what pensée!) La Re Qu'on Pense, wrote Harsnet. 'Ard Object, he wrote. Objet Dard. L'Entre Deux Verres, he wrote. Why do my titles come out better in French than in English? he wrote. Because I see it from the outside? Xenakis last night, he wrote. Picked him up at Imperial College. I gave them a three-hour lecture on the basic principles of stochastics, he said. Some composers today don't even understand the simple calculus, he said. Can you believe it? For him Stockhausen a child, Boulez a tyrant, Berio an entertainer. There is one artist in every generation whose work possesses real significance, he said. The rest is the chorus. In this generation it happens to be me. It's nothing to be proud of, just a fact. Unity in his mind of architecture, music, astronomy, geology. Tried to explain the real implications of quantum physics as we crossed Kensington Road. Cars honking everywhere. Then DNA. I told him it was the size of it all disturbed me. I kept seeing these double helices like two snakes winding up an invisible tree, only smaller. He scratched with his stick on the ground (we were in Hyde Park by this time). An attendant warned us not to deface public property. He urged me to come to Paris. The level of intellectual activity there. Sustained intellectual activity. He kept repeating: sustained intellectual activity. His

66

current work on the concept of flow with Thom and Deleuze. One to deal with its mathematical, one with its philosophical and psychoanalytic, one with its artistic implications. Huge Government grant. Research assistants. I told him all that left me cold. He looked at my pityingly, no doubt thinking that I was succumbing to the English diseases, amateurism and laziness. Everywhere he goes he leaves his umbrella behind. He's stuck a label on all his umbrellas with his name and address but he never gets them back. There are thieves everywhere, he said. Last week, sitting in the Luxembourg Gardens, he became aware of a pain in his foot. He took off his shoe to investigate, then heard a noise overhead and saw a flock of starlings flying past. Became fascinated by the pattern as they wheeled and changed direction. Got out paper and pencil to try and think through the implications of what he had just seen, then gave up and started off home. Some time later found he had only one shoe on. Went back but the other had gone. It's unbelievable the number of thieves there are, he said. Now planning huge work to take place simultaneously in every town in Greece and on every mountain. Not music but transformation of sound-waves already in the air. Perhaps colour-waves too, if technology ready in time. Twenty-four hours non-stop performance. After that plans similar experience world-wide. Perhaps to last a year. Once we have landed on Mars we will be able to beam it to the galaxy, he said. Speak to the entire galaxy and wait for replies. Complained of pains in his back. I wanted to give him supper but he said he would take sandwiches up to his room and get on with his work. Greece was waiting, he said. The world was waiting. At the desk asked if anyone had returned an umbrella, but the clerk shook his head. Asked to have breakfast brought up to his room at six. I work every day from 6.20 to 9.30 a.m., he said, and then from 4 p.m. to midnight if I can. I can work in any conditions, he said. Any conditions. I have my pocket calculator and there are always things which need doing for which there is no need for my big computer. At home though he can plug himself in to other computers all over the world. I work a lot with M.I.T., he said. And Stanford. Also links with Japan. Month in Kyoto every year with his wife. Apart from Paris Kyoto is the only city she likes, he said. The clerk then dug out an umbrella and showed it to him. It looks like mine, he said, examining it, but there's no label on it. He handed it back. You see what I mean? he said to me. I went home through the Park. Strong winds gusting up from the South. Branches down, the trees creaking. Flat reasonably quiet though. Sat and thought about Xenakis. How he was tortured in '44. He showed me the scars. I concentrated on the implications of Einstein's General Theory, he said, and on the pathos of his later career. So managed to get through without revealing anything. He walked through the mountains for seventy-two hours after escaping. My feet have never been the same since, he said. I have to take off my shoes whenever I can. Something still very wrong with the right hand side of the bottom panel. Sat through the night and looked at it. As usual the whole thing seemed immense. Much too big for my abilities. But gradually I calmed down. Lost my anxiety. It simply became a field of force, like any other. I began to see the dangers of overcrowding, over-invention. The most important thing in fact the clear glass. Never to forget that. But many of the elements still not relating. No proper tension between them. Better from the back. Thought again about possibility of having it viewable equally from front and back. No front and back, in other words. But again dismissed idea. Back should be seen as back. Outlines visible but surface different. The principle always that nothing should be hidden: There is only this. And yet that only should be able to stimulate dreams, create anxiety. So Harsnet. Is this all there is? Why no more? Why this? Why here? he wrote. Such questions should occur to the viewer, he wrote. And force him to ask the same questions of his life, and to reply: This is all there is and it is enough. Enough not because we must content ourselves with the minimum, he wrote, but because there is never more, if more means meaning, wholeness, salvation, redemption, all the rest. The glass itself must make that clear, he wrote. But tell story too, if viewer wants a story, a story about our desire for more and the folly of that desire, the desire for more and the inevitable frustration of that desire. Desire of Bride to be more than a bride, to be a mother too. Desire of Bachelors to be more than bachelors, to be husbands and fathers too. Hold up the glass to such viewers, wrote Harsnet (typed Goldberg), and let them see themselves in it. The bridge between the different elements that, between them, could add up to a story, is space, he wrote. Let those who will fall into that space, and fall for ever. The space is glass, he wrote. The whiteness of delirium, he wrote. The whiteness of real nothingness. Not the whiteness of the whale, which is still something, but the emptiness of the glass, which is nothing. The ordinary wall behind, he wrote, this wall and no other, these viewers and no others. And so on. And yet, he wrote, the wonder is that this nothing holds the elements together. So that they are and are not linked in their impossible non-consummation. And yet the drama lies in this, wrote Harsnet, that perhaps the Bride really wishes to remain only a bride, at the moment of her bridity, and the bachelors only bachelors, at the moment of their bachelorhood, dangling together like pegs on a line, boys together at eternal stag party, as the bride a virgin forever in her dream of giving herself up to something else, crossing the threshold to another existence. As we all of us want to escape ourselves and remain ourselves, want to leave ourselves behind and take ourselves with us, want the world transfigured and yet to remain ourselves in a transfigured world. The passage from the Virgin to the Bride a kind of death, he wrote, as is the passage from bachelor to husband. Rites of passage designed solely to make transition bearable, he wrote. But today? Can we still talk meaningfully of rite? Where is the threshold? he wrote. Are we inside already? Or forever outside? To change is to die, he wrote, but not to change is also to die. How to overcome Narcissism without self-destruction? he wrote. Kafka and the blood-soaked sheets, he wrote: horror and nostalgia both. Urge to build,

69

to make, as compensation for anxieties of exile, he wrote. Yet the more you build the greater the sense of exile. On and on, he wrote. On and on. It is not a question of whether it is better or worse to remain a virgin or a bachelor, he wrote, but rather of bringing the terror to the surface. The terror and the desire, he wrote. Kafka, he wrote. Always there waiting for me when I go deep enough. The horror of bachelorhood which condemns you to arid thought for ever, and the horror of marriage, which condemns you to lies and hypocrisy for ever. Art itself like marriage, he wrote, as Kafka understood, with its hypocrisy and lies, its myth of wholeness, its myth of meaning. But like bachelorhood too, with its arid cranking of the engine of thought, its empty impotence, its time drained of all meaning. The big glass, he wrote, as last work of art and first work of non-art. The big glass tells the story of the aridity of art, he wrote, of the lies of art, of the machine without the fuel to make it move. The big glass as icon of aridity, he wrote, and Goldberg, in the margin, *BG icon of aridity*. First the making of the glass, wrote Harsnet (and Goldberg typed), then the showing of the glass, and then the end. Après moi le tinkle of broken glass, wrote Harsnet. How could I ever have thought La Tartine d'Albertine would make a good title? he wrote. All right as name of café, but no more. The idea of a title, he wrote, implies an entity. But what is the entity in this case? Is it what is on the glass, or what is on the glass plus what is seen through the glass, or just the glass itself? Pseudo-excitation, he wrote. The Bride only pretends to be excited. The Bachelors only pretend to be thrilled. But how can we be sure? he wrote. It has all happened before, he wrote, and it will all happen again. There can be no title, he wrote, because there is no object. There can only be description, he wrote, The Big Glass. Litany of the chariot as it moves on its runners, he wrote. Litany of solipsism. Litany of onanism. No surprises, he wrote, no hope. The chariot moves back and forth, he wrote, but to no purpose. No heat is engendered, he wrote. Nothing happens. And that

70

is perhaps the way they all want it. For the cold is their element. Timelessness is their element. The hypothetical is their element. Even now, he wrote, with the first heat of early summer in the middle of London, even now, with all the windows open, the glass freezes the room. The sense of its otherness, he wrote, just as I wanted it, an alien object, one never before seen on our planet, not quite animal, not quite mineral, not quite vegetable, yet familiar, familiar. If only we could bring it into focus, he wrote, if only we could concentrate hard enough, we might be able to understand what it is. But the more we try the more the feeling of familiarity evaporates. Diana, he wrote. Hidden by her handmaids she is seen to blush, then turns to Actaeon and throws water in his face to blind him, to stop him seeing her naked, but that is not enough and she knows it is not enough, and soon he feels the horns growing on his forehead, *dat sparso capiti vivacis cornus cervis*, she caused to grow on his head the horns of the long-lived stag, as if the cost of seeing her naked had to be death, first metamorphosis then death. The question is, wrote Harsnet (typed Goldberg), does she entice him there or does he want to come? Does she entice him or does he appear by chance? Ovid refuses to answer, he wrote. For he says, while Titania is bathing there in her accustomed pool, lo! Cadmus' grandson, his day's toil deferred (*dilata parte laborem*), comes wandering through the unfamiliar woods with unsure footsteps (*per nemus ignotum non certis passibus errans*), and enters Diana's grove, for so fate would have it (*pervenit in locum: sic illum fata ferebant*). How easy, wrote Harsnet (typed Goldberg), it would have been to write: Lo, Cadmus' grandson enters Diana's grove, but no, Ovid defers the verb for a line and a half, telling us – what? That, his day's toil having been deferred, he wanders through unfamiliar woods with unsure footsteps. Yet where is this wandering taking him? Where are those unsure footsteps taking him? Where is the participle, seemingly indicating perpetual motion, *errans*, heading for? To Diana's grove! And why? For so fate would have it: *sic fata ferebant*. *Sic fata ferebant*, wrote

71

Harsnet. Inscribe in glass? The point is, he wrote (and Goldberg typed), that he had spent his life seeking her out, yet left his feet to do the dirty work. Would the outcome have been different had he acknowledged to himself what he was doing? he wrote. No, he wrote, because Diana herself does not acknowledge either that she has been waiting all her life for him to appear. That, he wrote, is the significance of the tell-tale blush. Red as the clouds which flush beneath the sun's slant rays, says Ovid, red as the rosy Dawn, were the cheeks of Diana as she stood there in view without her robes. She stood, Ovid tells us, turning aside a little, and cast back her gaze: *in latus obliquum tamen adstitit oraque retro.* And her only words to him are: Now you are free to tell that you have seen me all unrobed – if you can tell! – *nunc tibi me posito visam velamine narres, sit poteris narrare, licet!* The point is, wrote Harsnet (typed Goldberg), that Actaeon is not free to narrate what he has seen, but Ovid is. Actaeon is torn to pieces by his own dogs, but Ovid is not torn. That is the pathos of the narrative, he wrote. That he neither really sees nor is really torn, that he cannot enter the world of either comedy or tragedy, neither O brave new world that hath such people in it, nor Dark dark dark beneath the blaze of noon. Only the story, and after that another story, and another and another. Actaeon sees and Actaeon is torn, wrote Harsnet, but Ovid in his exile by the Black Sea neither sees the Goddess nor is torn by the dogs. For him, wrote Harsnet, there is only the endless metamorphosis of narrative, no end except for the non-end of his death. That is why only the glass will do it, wrote Harsnet. Only the glass will tell the story, the story of that story, the truth of that truth, the lie of that lie. That is why, he wrote, there have to be three stages, first the making of the glass, then the showing of the glass, and then the end. In the Middle Ages, he wrote, the glass in the cathedral walls glowed with the fires of judgement and damnation. The worshipper looked up and wondered. Through the glass shone God's sun, setting the colours alight: blue, green, yellow, red. The damned on Christ's left, the saved on His

72

right. Today, he wrote (and Goldberg typed), the glass will stand in a gallery, lit by artificial light, with no right and no wrong way of looking at it, no left and no right hand, no salvation or damnation. The relationship to images is destroyed, he wrote, when they are looked at only for themselves, gazed at only for themselves. The truth of the museum and the gallery is a lie, he wrote. Beauty is a lie. Verisimilitude is a lie. Masterpieces are a lie. Museums and galleries as false delay, he wrote. Delay of death, not delay of life, he wrote. But death can only be fought with death, and life with life, he wrote. Only the death of death, the unmasking of the lie of lies, he wrote. The glass stands silent in the gallery, he wrote, but it burns up the lies of the gallery. On the one hand, he wrote, it pushes nothing out of its way. On the other it burns up everything around it. On the one hand it is nothing and asks for nothing, on the other it is the secret and silent source of the destruction of everything. On the one hand it makes no demands, he wrote, on the other it is the vitriol which corrodes everything with which it comes into contact, the Gorgon which turns to stone all who gaze upon it. On the one hand, he wrote, it is like everything else in the gallery, on the other it is opposed to everything in the gallery. It is the one because it is the other, he wrote. It is malign because it is benign. It is unlike everything else and it is the cause of the destruction of everything else because it is no different from anything else. Once installed, he wrote, it will start to do its work, and it will go on doing it, in the day-time, in the night-time, in the midst of visitors and in the empty silence, when the mausoleum is open to the public and when the mausoleum is closed to the public. I will no longer be there, he wrote, but I will no longer be needed. It may take five years, he wrote, or it may take ten, or a hundred or a thousand, but sooner or later everything in the mausoleum will be affected and everything in all the other mausoleums in the city, and everything in all the other mausoleums in the country, and everything in all the other mausoleums in the world. And when its work is done, he wrote, it will grow quite transparent again and then it will disintegrate. Only the labels will be left, he wrote, for those who come after to examine and try to decipher, as sarcophagi and empty tombs are examined by archaeologists to try and determine who and what once lay inside them. There will be no flood, he wrote, and there will be no fire, but it will do its work. Negation, he wrote, once the attribute of the Devil, now the ally of the truth. And when the lies have gone, he wrote, when the mausoleums lie empty, then streams will once again begin to flow and trees to bud, mountains will raise their heads again and gales will turn into gentle breezes, while the sun will only warm and never scorch. Not rejection, he wrote, but seeming compliance. Not offended silence but seemingly grateful speech. The secret agent in his place, he wrote, the infiltrator safely ensconced. For the gesture of revolt begs for understanding. The gesture of rejection pleads mutely for forebearance. It asks for open vindication, he wrote, but I ask only to do my task. What must be done. In the night. In the mocking silence. Narrow horizons, he wrote. No favours. Head down. Keep going. Do not listen to the tempting voices. The voices which tell you to let go. To give up. To forget. To sleep. To leave it to the transforming imagination. All my life, he wrote, I have used art to fight against myself. To open up the darkness. To make hard what is soft. It had to come to this, he wrote. It had to come to the nightly struggle with the big glass, like the struggle with Proteus, who must be held no matter what form he takes, bull, bear, fox, fire, water. Not the strength of the body, he wrote, and not the strength of the will, but the strength of the whole self. For the body by itself is not enough, he wrote. The will by itself is not enough. You cannot will yourself to fight against the truth, he wrote. You cannot will yourself to hold out against reality. If you do that, he wrote, then sooner or later the will will crack and the truth will emerge, reality will re-assert itself. Only if the whole person is engaged, he wrote, only if you have the sense that the truth, in however paradoxical a form, is on your side, that reality, no matter how disguised, is what

74

you are working towards, only then will Proteus be defeated. Not killed, not annihilated, but held fast and made to talk. Kafka, he wrote. Bonnard. Vermeer. Stravinsky. Wittgenstein. We each have our pantheon, he wrote. We each have our team. For we need all the help we can get. Those for whom the whole self is at stake, he wrote. Not the preachers. Not the ranters. Not the inspired madmen. Not the dull conformists. Not the poised ironists. Not the all-knowing nihilists. Not those who swear only by theory or those who swear only by practice. Not the splashers on of paint and not the witty designers of operatic sets, not those who claim to have their fingers on the pulse of things and not those who shut themselves up and ignore the world. Not those, but the few who respect silence, who respect the world, who are prepared to listen, who are prepared to change, who are aware of human weakness and vulnerability, who are aware of the imperatives of life and the imperatives of the work in hand. So Harsnet. And Goldberg, pursing his lips in concentration, flicking the hair out of his eyes, typed furiously on. And all this, wrote Harsnet (typed Goldberg), in spite of the awareness, always present, sometimes blinding, of the long perspective, the common fate of all, the eventual overheating of the universe or its eventual overcooling, the end of everything. Imagine an ant, he wrote, crawling up the legs of a table. What sense of the table does it have? Not ours, surely. Does it have a sense of four legs, of the function of the surface? And imagine us in our world as ants on the leg of a table. Who knows but that it may look very different to bigger, different beings? Another dimension, or at least our world as a single dimension among many, he wrote. But how to convey this? How to make the viewer perceive this? Velasquez, he wrote. The point of view in *Las Meninas*. Cucumbers, he wrote. Tomatoes. Cauliflower if fresh and firm. Lemon. Olives. Cream cheese. Bread. Two years, he wrote. Two years since I started on the big glass. Two years since I set up the glass and started to make marks on it. The way it advanced, he wrote. So much done so quickly and then nothing. And

75

then a quick advance again and then again nothing. And then the mistakes, he wrote. And again the swift advance. When it is done, he wrote, it should look as though it had always been there. Remove all traces of process, he wrote. Let it not bear the traces of work, the traces of time. Shadow of reality, he wrote, yet itself reality too. Not depiction of a bride, he wrote, but bride herself. Not depiction of alchemical process, but process itself. First *calcinatio*, he wrote, then *leukosis* leading to *iosis*. Celebration of Red (Solar) King and White (Lunar) Queen. White Queen as Hanged Lady, he wrote. Celebration of union of Earth and Sky, he wrote. Each confined to own domain, he wrote. Union cannot take place. Yet at the same time mere *graffito* in *pissoir*, he wrote. The glass as a part of my life, he wrote, as a culmination of my life. The word cannot be spoken, he wrote. Signs to be read only after I am gone: Know only that a message was sent. The truth of the matter, he wrote, is that no one wants to be rescued. We like our desert island too much. We enjoy sending out our messages in bottles too much. But at the same time we do want to be saved. And so on. Something about that visit to the oculist in Salisbury with Marcus, he wrote. Something about those magnifying glasses laid out in rows. Embed magnifying glass in lower right hand? he wrote. Not hole to see through but glass to alter vision? Or just attach to big glass? (For viewer to use if and when he wants.) That visit to the Prado, he wrote. Taxi from airport. Straight inside. Up huge stone stairs. Sounds of children playing round corners. As in Louvre. Those huge rooms. High ceilings. Echos. Straight through to *Las Meninas*. The size of it. Nothing had prepared me for that. Photos never give any sense of size. For that you have to be up against the real thing. Let the eye move over it. Swivel the head. That combination of family snap and Last Judgement. Oh my. Farewell to picture as repository of meaning, welcome to picture as representation. Farewell without nostalgia. Welcome without enthusiasm. Just the way it has to be. No more. No less. My pathetic attempt to combine snapshot and Last Judgement in early picture of God and his family, God in suit with cigar, Mary, white hair, Joseph ditto, child Jesus playing with dove, sailor suit. First time theme of picture excited me though. Don't know why. Some sort of tension I suppose. What people objected to in the end was not God, as I'd thought, but the suburban house in the background and the garden out of House and Garden. Taxi then from Prado and night train up to Léon. Sometimes half an hour is enough. Enough for a lifetime. What was I reading then? Waiting in Madrid Station buffet? *Pierrot mon ami?* Feel it in my hands still, the little livre de poche edn. The great thing is to keep your hands clean. Not add to the pollution. The evasions of someone like Goldberg. The hypocrisies. The self-deceptions. I love you but I love her more. The dictates of the heart. Leaving the children will destroy me. But then living with her is destroying me. You don't know what it means. And when I'm with the other I just feel myself to be a better person. She makes me discover things in myself I didn't know were there. That can't be all bad, can it? It must mean something, mustn't it? So he thinks of himself as a warm-hearted, caring human being. An upright man. Which in a sense he is. But always this trail of slime. A week's good work and then a week of drought, wrote Harsnet. That seems to be the pattern. But no easier to deal with for that reason. When that happens, he wrote, I don't just feel I'm not moving forward, I feel I'm sliding right back. That if I'm not going forward I'm going back. My body just won't respond to the glass. Nor my mind. I get nothing from it. I look at it and I don't even see it. Sense of unease, he wrote, growing quickly into sense of revulsion. Pain in the stomach, he wrote. Not just at contemplation of the glass but at the thought of its being here, in the flat, with me. Not only revulsion, he wrote, but a sense of indignity. Of shame. As though its presence in some way accused me. As though my relationship to it dirtied me. Not the desire to destroy it, but rather to turn time back and let me never have been involved with it. I can hardly bear to enter the room where it stands, he wrote. Even the flat. I loiter about outside, remember unnecessary errands. All the time I would like to be somewhere else, someone else. But I'm not. I'm me. I can't escape it. It contaminates my sleep. It destroys my digestive system. How has this happened? Why is it doing this to me? Not despair at failure. That is bearable. It suggests that next time, with a little more luck, or hard work, success may come. No. It is much more physical than that. Revulsion as the most basic of the instincts. Revulsion at the thought that I am responsible for it. At the thought that I could ever have imagined it had any value. Stomach turning over, he wrote. Sense of degradation. But why? Because I have wasted my time with something like that? But how else should I have spent my time? Sense that in spite of everything it too only adds to the stream of lies and filth? That I too have done my little bit for pollution? And I dared to condemn Goldberg. And Hilda. Madge. Helen. At least they never pretended to be pure. A feeling, wrote Harsnet, such as I have never experienced before, not so much of wishing I had never been born, as never been born as me. And the feeling of this as the ultimate sin against the Holy Ghost. The reason destroying it now would be no solution, he wrote, is that what sickens me is not the object itself but the time and thought I have put into it. Be very clear, he wrote: I do not feel that it is time and thought wasted because the end result is less than I had hoped. But rather that the time and thought put into it had somehow polluted me. That can never be destroyed. Denied. The nights spent in the room under the cold fluorescent light. The careful compiling of the notes for the box. Why? For what? The question I return to, he wrote (and Goldberg typed), is always the same: I put everything into this, every-thing I had by way of mind and body and heart, and this is what I have produced. Does this then reveal to me what I am? No more excuses, I said at the start. If I am to live by that, he wrote, then this represents all I am capable of. The best of me. This rubbish. This trash. Who will absolve me now? I want it to be as though I had never been. I want it to be as though I had never taken that turning. But that cannot be. There it is. Ocular proof. The irony of my vision of the glass burning up the rest of the exhibits in the gallery in which it is housed, when here it is, burning up everything around it in this flat, burning me up. So Harsnet. And Goldberg in the margin: *Despair. Self-hatred.* Days, wrote Harsnet, since I last entered the room. Days spent staring at the wall. Days since I opened this notebook. Horror of the summer noises in the street. Horror of the dogs running on the Common. Days eating scraps because I could not bear to enter a shop, talk to another human being, have people see me. Tried working through the Alekhine Paz had given me, but even chess filled me with disgust. Yet a kind of relief now at writing all this down. Yesterday I couldn't have done it. Couldn't have picked up the pen and opened the notebook and faced the blank page. Does my writing this down now mean that I am a little bit reconciled to myself? Those words of Kafka's, which have never ceased to haunt me: Where does the strength come from to write: I have no strength any more? The question he is really asking, I think, wrote Harsnet (typed Goldberg), is this: Is that secret strength a minus or a plus? One more temptation or the start of a recovery? Will it ever be given us to know? How many bad paintings, books, pieces of music we owe to this final, mysterious strength, he wrote. How many banal and clumsy, weak and foolish artists have justified their work as that which saved them from despair. Is that a reason to dismiss them or their claims? Not dismiss, wrote Harsnet (typed Goldberg). I merely state the facts. Fortunately, he wrote, while every person, more or less, in the Western world, has access to pen and paper and can write down a word or two, few will turn as naturally to painting or music to soothe their troubled breasts. Some consolation, he wrote. My loathing of terms like depression and despair, he wrote. Not that buoyant optimism much better. Yesterday able to enter the room once more, he wrote. Not easy, but I was able to do it. The physical revulsion gone at least. As always, amazed at the size of it, nine feet high and six across. Approached it as lovers approach each other after a quarrel, waiting to see how it would respond. Could not stay long in the room with it, but the ice had been broken. Could at least think about it, visualize it again, if not with pleasure, at least not with that sick-making horror of the past few weeks. How everything stopped. Even this notebook. How I slept too much, and less and less well of course, but the truth was I did not want to wake up. How the days, instead of each being distinct from each other, merged into each other. May all that be behind me. Another week gone by, he wrote. Any idea that the bout of despair was over was quickly dispelled as the old horror came over me again in waves. Dragged myself to the doctor who told me I had to expect such things at my age and prescribed vitamin pills. I thanked him and tore up the prescription at the door. But last two days a little better. Perhaps I tried to force the pace. Perhaps I should simply have left it alone for a while. But alone to do what? Either I work on the big glass, he wrote, or my life is not worth living. Easy to see what effect sudden nausea at even the thought of the big glass would have on a life lived in this way. But that is how it is. No doubt if I had responded to Hilda and Annie and the rest as they told me I should respond, as they all told me my true nature, my deeper nature was crying out to respond, I would be surrounded today by love and wives and children and the rest. Goldberg a living example of the folly of such dreams, he wrote. Not so much the compromises, the deceits, the hypocrisies affecting his work, his women, his children, even his friends, but the sense of deapair and failure hovering over him, as though he was trapped and didn't know how it had happened or what he should or could do. So Harsnet. And Goldberg, pushing the typewriter from him, dragging the pad towards him, Dear Harsnet, I am well aware of the fact that you have cut yourself off from all your old friends, and that you wish to have nothing more to do with them. You will recall, however, that before you vanished from our lives you entrusted me with the notes you had kept while working on the Big Glass and the Green Box, telling me I could do what I liked with them, and adding, in your usual sensitive way, that I could always use them to wipe my arse if the paper decided to sack me and I found myself really hard up. As I wrote to you at the time (since you refused even then to see me or any of your old friends and supporters) I accepted the MS as a sacred trust and would do what I could to see that it eventually saw the light of day in the most appropriate form. I had thought at the time, wrote Goldberg, turning the page, wiping his brow, taking a sip of orange juice from the glass on the desk beside him, dreaming for a moment of the cigarettes he had given up two years earlier, I had thought, he wrote, that an edited version of the text, with only those comments directly concerned with the Big Glass included, would serve you best. I had to put the project aside for a while, he wrote, as the rent had to be paid, not to speak of alimony, school fees and the rest, and, coming back to it after a considerable period, much longer, unfortunately, than I had anticipated, and I will not even try to apologize since you gave me a completely free hand – anyway, he wrote, trying to ignore the damp spots left on the page of his pad by his sweaty hands, anyway, coming back to it after all that time I realized that it would be quite impossible in practice to separate the valuable and the worthless, the public and the private, and that, in a sense, one would have to think in terms of either publishing the whole thing *exactly as it stood*, or not doing it at all. Though there is a good deal there which I found deeply offensive, he wrote, as you must have realized when you sent me the stuff, though, knowing you as I do, I suspect it may not even have crossed your mind, anyway, to be brief, I have, of course, put my feelings to one side and decided to honour the integrity of. Pushing the pad aside he returned to his typing. But is that not what he wanted? he typed (as Harsnet had written). Do not most of us search for excuses most of the time? Excuses not to do the work we think we might or should do, excuses not to be kind or considerate or whatever it is we feel we should be? What he wanted, wrote Harsnet (typed Goldberg) and what I wanted. The difference is that I knew what I wanted and he did not. Though, wrote Harsnet, that difference may not be as great as I sometimes imagine. For what does know mean in such cases? What does want mean? Everything a substitute for everything else, he wrote. Migration of desire, he wrote. Migration of meaning. Never where you think it is. Only traces left. Footprints. Fingerprints. Glass as trace of a fourth dimension, he wrote. Oculist charts at bottom right hand? he wrote. Not hole. Not magnifying glass, but oculist charts. My unease at having to cut into the glass, at having to add to the glass, he wrote. Yet my sense that that was the place for a transformation of vision. If top panel is without perspective and bottom is nothing but perspective, then is that not the place for a different kind of vision? Oculist charts the answer? Distinct from flatness of top and from perspective of bottom, he wrote. Three types of projection then, he wrote, to go with the three rollers on the grinder, the three draft pistons, the three times three malic moulds, the three times three shots. Three oculist charts, he wrote. Place on top of each other in different perspective from rest of panel. Slices of invisible column, he wrote. Or sense of circles moving away from us. Incise straight onto the glass, he wrote. The idea of the witnesses keeps alive the detective story element in my work, he wrote, and especially in the big glass. Private eye and myths of sky and earth, he wrote. Philip Marlowe and Actaeon. As always, he wrote, painting lags behind literature, which saw the connection as long ago as Poe. Painting nearly always fifty years or even a hundred behind the times. The world of Grosz for instance. Gives the impression of being so contemporary but really plays out themes of nineteenth century, badies, goodies, etc. Why we feel comfortable with such art, however grotesque, whereas the greatest art always leaves us a little bit uncomfortable, as though the earth we stood on had given a sudden lurch. A murder has been committed, wrote Harsnet (typed Goldberg). A bride has been killed. Unfulfilled desire roams unchecked, lacking a clear origin or goal. Civil servant who cut up the boys he lured back to his house, burned the pieces, buried them. Smell alerted the neighbours who suspected faulty sewers. Woman abducted on motorway in broad daylight while phoning AA. Later murdered. Man going berserk in Surrey commuter town, gunning down thirty. The fruits of peace. Launderette yesterday, he wrote. Two women. Wait till I catch up with him. I'll show him what it means to walk out on his family. I'll cut him up small and fry him for the kids' breakfast. And on the bus: Every morning he comes out into the garden with his cup of tea and stands there, looking round. I can see him from the kitchen window you see. Every morning it's just the same routine. He comes out into the garden and sips his tea and looks around. Sometimes he looks straight at me. He can't see me of course but it makes me feel funny. Sometimes he walks slowly over and inspects one of his plants. I never liked the look of him. Work out double perspective, wrote Harsnet. Select charts. Find method of incising. And Goldberg in the margin: *Oculist charts*. Still a kind of fear, wrote Harsnet (and Goldberg, sighing, typed). Fear that all this may just be in my head. Fear that when I finally go in and face it, ready to start, the old revulsion will rise up in me again. Fear that I have only dreamed of moving forward, that when I go in and face it I will see that it is a mistake, not possible, uninteresting. That it was never on. Stay with it, he wrote. The important thing is to stay with it. The closer I get to completion the more I dread it, he wrote. Why? The more there is to go wrong, of course. When you start there is a sense in which everything you do is right, there is no clear sense of wrong, though of course it is here that you may make the inevitable false move, take the inevitable wrong turning. But this will only emerge much later. At the time all is sweetness and light. By now I have already committed myself to so much, he wrote. It is myself in there. Myself I am afraid to face. Myself without excuses. Myself after trying my hardest for three whole years. Is this all you have to show for it? he wrote. Is this what you imagined the culmination of your life would be? Until now I could always say: this is trivial, not important, but tomorrow

I'm starting the big one. But now I have started it, am well on with it, this is it, this is me, no avoiding the fact. Is this then all you are? All you want? I have to say yes because there is nothing else. I have done what I wanted, or thought I wanted, I have pushed as hard as I could, and this is it. No alibi. I was not elsewhere. I was here. It was not someone else. It was me. I did it. Is this then the last temptation? he wrote. To say: Only this? After all, he wrote, who am I to judge? Only? he wrote. Why only? Because that's what it feels like today, he wrote, and because I know in my heart of hearts that it will feel like that tomorrow as well. Limit the horizons, he wrote. Keep going. Figure out how to incise the charts. Think of that corner of the glass. The blind king led by his daughter. After that he is on his own. Just the three parts of the project, he wrote: the finishing of the glass, the showing of the glass, and the end. So Harsnet. Work on the charts progressing, he wrote. Working on negative, scraping away silver. Slow, he wrote, but I like it like that. The slower the better, he wrote, since one of the problems is the speed with which it could all be over. It is beginning to transform the rest, he wrote. The contiguous circles to be read as either columnar or flat. Whichever way, a new perspective is introduced into lower panel. Starting to make bachelor apparatus interesting again, as I hoped it might. My old dream, he wrote: get away from agony of background-foreground and from the over-assertiveness usually involved in destruction of that relationship. Get away from perpetual need to fill in, fill up, he wrote. With us since Giotto, he wrote. Yet while empty part of wall or canvas feels sloppy, unfinished, this is not the case with the glass. Here transparency is benign. What floats onto it floats onto it. Basta. Good work the past few nights, he wrote. Very hot. Windows wide open. Drunken shouts from street, Common. Peace. Not that terrible assertion of the self, of what the self sees or imagines it sees or just sees in imagination. Not that terrible sense of showing off. Art as aggression, he wrote. You will see it my way. Look how clever, profound, etc. I am. Admire. Pay. Etc. All that gone with

84

glass, he wrote. The open window, he wrote. The glass on which objects float, mingling with the wall behind. If you want a story, you can have one. If not, not. If you want to walk round it, you can do so. If you want to get on with more important things, nothing stops you. If you want to watch your reflection pacing beside you, there it is. A narrative, he wrote. Or a poem. Or an enigma. Yesterday, he wrote, it started to dance for me again. I did not look at the rest of it, deliberately. But could feel it all. Sense of its presence, he wrote, but not an oppressive presence (as with *For Micah*, for example). Benign? he wrote. Perhaps. Sense of buoyancy. Forget titles, he wrote. Big glass is enough. Big drinker. Big dipper. But telescope not far away too. Try saying big glass as you would say big game and then as you would say big deal. At last lower panel taking shape, he wrote. Beginning to think now of boxing match in upper panel right. Gone back to old sketches. Problem is to balance movement of chariot (with its solipsistic litany). In pub today, big fight on TV. Fifteen dreary rounds. No electricity. Two tired men holding on to each other to stop themselves falling down. And referee trying to prize them apart, to keep at least the pretence of a fight going. Audience booing. My old dream of a play set in a boxing-ring, he wrote. The ape-devil who bangs his drum and shouts: Comedy! Tragedy! Melodrama! And the six (or eight) who carry out his instructions. Six-minute *Hamlet*, etc. How he stops them. Starts them again. Slows them down. Speeds them up. Gets them to repeat moments he likes. How they gradually pull away from him. Carry out his orders with more and more reluctance. How he grows angry. Then mad. Tries to force them into position. They go limp. Then turn on him. Destroy him. Mechanical operation of the spirit. And my other dreeam: Eight foot high puppet Clytemnestra and ten-foot Agamemnon. Reduplicated in three-foot puppets, on wheels, on rails running round auditorium. She chases him round and round. Up goes the axe. Down goes the axe. Three times I am struck, alas alas. And Cassandra hooting and howling. The chariot goes back and forth, back and forth, chanting its litany, he wrote. The water-mill goes round and round. The chocolate-grinder grinds and grinds. The scissors snip and snip. Bring boxing-match down to top edge of lower panel? he wrote. My feeling now that top panel should not be touched. How it grew upon me in the night, he wrote. Even at the cost of dropping duck-rabbit effect and cast shadows. Everything suddenly fluid again, he wrote. As though those charts have opened up the glass, made everything start to live once more. Must take care, he wrote. What is there is there. Too much gone through to go back now. And yet? The longing to start again. No, he wrote. Forward is the only way. If there was ever a time to change things radically that time has long passed. And I would not give another year of my life to a new version, he wrote. I knew when I first thought of it, he wrote, when I first set it up, that it was to be the final piece. I knew once I started that there would be no going back. Doubts now only the result of panic, he wrote. Of the sense that perhaps everything needs rethinking, that perhaps next time I might get it right. That is the difference, he wrote, between me and Goldberg, me and McGrindle and the rest. They can always start again and it doesn't matter. Even Bacon can destroy what he doesn't like and start again. But if you can start again it means you have not even begun. I have begun, wrote Harsnet. Time has closed again behind me. What is there is there. Put aside thoughts of altering, he wrote. Time will tell. Not me. I will not be there to hear it. Began to see last night, he wrote, that duck-rabbit effect only variant on boxing-match. And anyway that area in danger of getting too cluttered. The glass needs to breathe, he wrote. You have to dare to let it breathe. You have to listen to the nature of its breathing. The rhythm of its breathing. The hardest thing, he wrote, is not to go on and on. Lévi-Strauss on primitive need to cover whole surface, he wrote. Ping-pong not boxing? he wrote. Analyse, analyse, he wrote. Then follow your instinct. Letter from Moira Fielding, he wrote. Wants to come and see glass. Organizing British show at Edinburgh Festival next year. Is this the right venue? Why not? he wrote. Lunch with Brian, he wrote. Incontinent dog. Has to walk after him with little trowel and paper bag. Writing television series dramatizing life of Jane Austen. Filled me with depression. Perhaps ask Goldberg over to see glass. May help resolve remaining problems. Ping-pong no solution. Tried moving to right but then too close to frame. But oculist charts perfect. Sat and glowed with satisfaction for a few hours in silence, studying their effect. How they play against wall and wainscoting behind. Impossible to reconcile space suggested by charts and space of room, which is just what I wanted, but for so long didn't know how to arrive at. The nights spent scraping away the silver backing among the best in my whole life, he wrote. Nothing but the sound of the scraper and the joy of uncovering. Yet none of that nonsense about Michelangelo and the stone. In the end a false and depressing view of what man is and can be. Mine the art of the cripple, the retarded, the autistic, not the beautiful and whole. For who is beautiful and whole? Nineteenth century tries to stifle doubts by crushing you with sheer bulk, he wrote. I want my doubts to play and dance. And Goldberg, drawing his pad towards him: The very words he used to excuse his behaviour at the wedding. It did not pacify Madge, he wrote, and when he told her they could have another go at it the following month she told him she had had enough. It didn't stop her hoping, waiting and hoping, for the next five years, he wrote, wasting her life when it was obvious he had no intention of going through with it. Dear Harsnet, he wrote, I am well aware of the fact that for some years now you have cut yourself off from your past and not deigned to reply to the letters of your friends, or even to return their calls, taking refuge in your answering machine and pretending not to be in when they rang at the bell. However, I have now been through the notebook you left with me and there are a few things I wish. Dear Harsnet, he wrote, it has taken me longer than I had at first anticipated to work my way through the manuscript you. Ping-pong doubles match perhaps? wrote Harsnet (and Goldberg set to typing again). Relate to

87

hypothetical activity of roller, grinder, sieves and mill, he wrote. Moira Fielding, he wrote. She stood at the door and stared. I told her she was the first person to see it since I started work on it. I watched her with interest but felt nothing. Completely detached, for some reason. She tried to be casual. Reeled off list of recent purchases by Scottish National Gallery of Modern Art: Paolozzi, Bacon, Kitaj, Freud, Hockney, Rauschenberg, Stella, Baselitz. Plans to make next year's show at the Festival the biggest ever in Britain of British art. Glass would have pride of place, she said. If I finish it, I said. If you finish it, she said. So second step taken care of, though first not yet completed. Letter from her later about possible purchase. Long way to go, I wrote back. Told her I might decide to scrap the whole thing. But I no longer believe that myself. Know it's too far advanced, must make its own way from now on. Perhaps ask Goldberg in to test his reactions. It will have to be installed either by a window or in the middle of the largest room you've got, I told her. I can see just where it will go, she said. Life has to be going on on both sides of it, I told her. She said she understood. Promised to send me photos of the gallery. It's very special, she said. For past few nights: struggle with ping-pong idea. No solution. Reverted to box-ing-match. As so often, first idea best, though you only discover that when you've decided to discard it and try something else. But tension starting to drain out of whole thing. As though now I know it will get done it is already in the past. Air less thin in the room. Sense of glass expanding as I enter. Almost of it rising to meet me. No longer that fear, that ice round my heart and in the pit of my stomach. But that is the inevitable second phase. I have been at this job long enough, wrote Harsnet (typed Goldberg), to know in advance what the different phases will be. The second phase is: familiarity, friendliness. Wait for the third, he wrote, for the return of otherness, oddity, spikiness. Allowed my eyes to wander over the whole of it, he wrote, and almost with satisfaction. At least without pain. Sure to feel again soon that I've botched it. My last chance and I've made a mess of it. But may have been through that earlier. Decided on 300 as optimum print run for notes to go in Green Box. A hundred to send out to specific individuals and institutions. Two hundred to make their own way in the world. Sense of pleasure at thought of someone trying to imagine glass only from notes in Green Box. From detailed descriptions of elements out of which it has been made. From biographies of the separate items: the glass, the frame, the wire, the paint. In Buenos Aires perhaps, or Kinchasa. Destroy glass and leave only box? A kind of solution, he wrote. But why not let glass make its own way? To destroy perhaps to attach too much importance to it. To suggest that it is worth the effort of destruction. Actually, he wrote, more difficult to destroy now than myself. Literally, of course, not metaphorically. Moses and the Golden Calf, he wrote. First break in pieces. Then pulverize. Then strew on water and make the people drink. What energy, he wrote. What anger. Now, he wrote, it is in a little room in a nondescript Victorian terraced house in a side-street in South London. Then it steps out into the world. No fanfares. Let it make its way or not, as fate determines. First the making of the glass, as I always planned, he wrote. Then the public exhibition of the glass. And finally, for me, the end. So my life: before glass, with glass, end. The king is dead, long live the king. But still a long way to go. The bride complete. Two-dimensional reproduction of three-dimensional shadow of four-dimensional creature. Milky Way complete too. And the three screens for the projection of the Bride's message. Goldberg delighted when I told him about the gauze and the draught, he wrote. Milky Way and Oculist Witnesses give me most satisfaction, he wrote. No element in glass to rest on my own arbitrary decision alone, he wrote. Central principle. That is the trouble with the boxing-match, he wrote. Why it won't get going. My arbitrary decision to hang up gauze and let draught play on it, but not my decision what the result of that play would be. Shape dictated by draught, he wrote, as configuration of oculist witnesses dictated by perspective. So the central principle of the glass: find the rules to work by and then stick to them. But that has always been my way, he wrote. Hence revulsion at brush. Too much dependent on hand, eye, mind. No. I knew I was on the right track when I felt that thrill of pleasure at <u>placing</u> object, not <u>painting</u> it. Each element nothing in itself, but whole more than sum of parts, he wrote. (Yet beauty of glass is that the story it tells is that the parts cannot cohere, cannot form a whole, <u>even though</u> <u>they would like to</u>.) That is why it had to be big. And from the start both divided and joined: two panels, one frame, yet each panel also enclosed in its own frame. The questioning of <u>boundaries</u>. The questioning of <u>limits</u>. Failure of shots to take effect, he wrote. Time spent looking for toy cannon. Fun of firing paint-soaked matches. Yet terrible weakness of final effect. The dots could have been made in other ways, and hardly noticeable anyway. Nothing in the final results leads you to sense of how it was achieved. Not true of rest. Once chosen, sense of uniqueness adheres to each element, each effect. Resonance of result, as one plays against other and eye moves across and round and up and down. One could easily get lost in there forever, Moira F. said. That is why it needs to be transparent, I said. A background of the ordinary. Of trees growing in a garden outside window. Of people walking about a room. And so on. Otherwise perhaps too dangerous. I don't want anyone to get lost in it, I said. To be unable to get back. Only I do want effect of <u>possibility</u> of getting lost. I think she understood. Death, wrote Harsnet (typed Goldberg). Going under ground, as the Greeks said. I think of it more as a diving into still water. Most marks for smallest splash. My recurring thought, he wrote: that the big glass will only start to breathe when I am gone. There is not enough room in the world for the two of us, he wrote. Set it on its feet, he wrote, and then let it go. Picasso. And Goldberg in the margin: *for the whole of the time I knew him he had, stuck on his studio wall, a reproduction of Picasso's amazing 1943 painting of the mother teaching her child to walk. That's not only what life is all about, he would say, pointing to it, it's what art's all about too*. You dive in, wrote Harsnet (typed Goldberg), and the water closes over you. Silence. But something is at work in the world. Something is on the move in the world. In a bookshop in Reykjavik someone buys a copy of the Green Box. Lovers meet in front of the big glass. I am not talking about the long run, he wrote. I have said enough about the long run already, where there will be no more Reykjavik and no more big glass and not even any more lovers. I am only talking about the next hundred years, he wrote, perhaps even only the next decade. But it can only happen, he wrote, if it is totally and utterly divorced from me. As though I had never been. A little fuss at the time cannot be avoided, he wrote, that is obvious. Whether I destroy the clothes first or fold them neatly the papers will have to have their story. But that will soon be forgotten. Only the glass will remain. Goldberg delighted, he wrote. Told him only Moira F. had seen it so far. He wanted to rush round straight away but I asked him to be patient. Socks, he wrote. Pullover (M&S). Tea. Moira F. on phone. I reminded her how fragile it was. She will send her best men down. It may not be ready in time, I told her, there's still a long way to go. The year after then, she said. Keep working. As if I needed any incentive. Area of boxing-match and duck-rabbit refuses to resolve itself. Is the problem that it is too much like a repetition of other areas of the glass? The glider for instance? Pleased with the way dust has settled on the sieves. The difficult calculations there beginning to pay off. Though my early dream of cones directly related to moulds and maintained in course of 180° rotation had to be abandoned. But enough survives. And dust really beginning to look good. Blissful week, he wrote. And Goldberg, in the margin: *sieves, dust*. Strange how certain areas seem to call out to me, wrote Harsnet, and working on them doesn't seem like work at all, more like simply breathing. So tired, he wrote. My plan of writing in here every day after night of work on glass and green box beginning to crumble. Forty months of non-stop work on one project beginning to take its toll. End seems as far away as ever, he wrote, with the whole of the lower right panel still to sort out. I was never in any hurry though, he wrote. I always knew it would take time. Mistake was perhaps to let Moira F. see it at this stage, he wrote. All those people wear me out. Nothing but running around and organizing. Organizing, he wrote. When the history of our times comes to be written, They Organized Themselves to Death will be the only possible epitaph. No doubt they mean well where the arts are concerned, he wrote, but for that reason they are the biggest menace. No doubt they think they have the interests of the artist at heart, he wrote, but for that reason they must be avoided like the plague. No doubt they see themselves as devoted middlewomen, bringing the truly important work of the time to the avid masses, but all they are really doing, wrote Harsnet (typed Goldberg) is fucking up the lives of both sets of people. They bring time into what is essentially timeless, he wrote. They bring anxiety about venues and dates into what is essentially a calm and anxiety-free activity. They try to ram down the throat of the public what the public quite rightly does not want. The Arts Council should be abolished, he wrote. And the Royal Arts Fund. And the Royal Literary Society. And the Royal Ballet. And the Royal Academy. Especially the Royal Academy, he wrote, with its Presidents and its Private Views and its Signed Goblets and its Concerts of Spanish music to go with the Murillo exhibition and its Concerts of Russian music to go with its Tatlin exhibition and its Concerts of Dutch music to go with its de Hooch exhibition, and its Silk-screened Scarves and its Special Offers and its Jigsaws of the Raft of Medusa and La Grande Jatte and its Good Taste and its Tondo and its Education Department and its Restaurant with its Tasty Snacks and its Cold Buffet and its Glass of Wine and its Napkins Designed by a Living Artist, and its Proximity to Cork Street, with its Galleries and their Private Views and their Favoured Clients and their Phone Calls to New York and their Summer Shows and their Autumn Shows and their Winter Shows and their Embossed Invitations and their Highly Polished Floors. There is no end to it all, wrote Harsnet (typed Goldberg). When you begin to think about it you grow dizzy, your stomach turns over, not just at the commercialism of it all, but at the aestheticism of it all, not just at the chequebooks but at the Intelligent Conversations, not just at the fifty percent but at the Sensitive Responses, not just at the winks and nods but at the Hushed Silence in the Presence of Art. Our civilization will be destroyed, he wrote, not by the Bomb but by its reverence for the Creative Spirit. Better never enter a church, he wrote, than enter in a spirit of false awe. Churches and art galleries, he wrote. That funereal atmosphere. False awe in the face of death, he wrote. No one knowing how to react, all speaking in low tones with solemn faces. It is the same with art, he wrote. Now even artists work with awed expressions, he wrote. Talk in whispers. Ape the critics. Ape the dealers. Ape the organizers. True art as a release from Art, he wrote. The glass as freedom, not constraint. As mirror of reality, not Monument to Creativity. None the less, he wrote, I should not have let her see it. Goldberg here last night, he wrote. Fatter and more unhealthy-looking than ever. Black circles round his eyes. Collar invisible in folds of neck. Patting his cheeks with his handkerchief all the time (till I asked him to stop it). Usual stories about true love at last. About need to pay for daughter's education. You don't know how much a growing girl needs, etc. Monograph on Motherwell to pay for year's schooling. Article on Schoenberg and the Expressionist Ethos. Yet the old seriousness still there, and the old laughter. Asked to be left alone with the glass for a while. So left him and walked down to the river. Dirt everywhere. Old newspapers. London now part slum part consumer paradise. Bellow when last here: A playground for the rich. Monte-Carlo on the Thames. Convinced that Chicago better because abattoir still functions. Won't be contradicted. Israel a disaster. French writing a disaster. Academies a disaster. Thought of him tonight as I walked down to the river. His romantic idea that gangsters closer to reality than the rest of us. And, since he's friendly with a few, he too closer,

93

etc. Preserve me from the self-confidence of a famous late middle age. The myth of the immigrant kid. The myth of the reality of power. American belief that the more you experience the more human you are, and that experience means pain, ecstasy, etc. Hadn't thought about him for years. The stink of hops hanging in the air, wafted over from Wandsworth breweries. Motorbikes lining the road by the hot-dog stall. Police waiting in the shadows. Traffic streaming non-stop over the bridge. Beautiful sense of anonymity. As if now Goldberg is in the room with the glass I no longer exist. Joy as sheet of old newspaper whirled across the road and wrapped itself round my leg. I looked down. It was my leg all right, but somehow detached from me. Or I was detached from it. After that, strangely, for the first time began to feel the glow of achievement. Not satisfaction at quality of whatever I had done, but simply at having done it at all. Having stuck at it. Something as big as that. As ambitious. Joy that my own hands had done it. Something that could never be undone, only destroyed outright. Sense that if I could let Goldberg see it there must be something there to see. Still much to do, but main task done. The leg that had stopped the newspaper had borne me up. The hands in my pockets had measured and scraped, put on and taken off. Something which had not been there three years ago now existed. Yet that something not so much a <u>thing</u> as an <u>eye</u>. Not so much an eye as a <u>template</u>. Or perhaps a lens. Shook newspaper off and the <u>wind</u> sent it whirling into the railings of the Park. Motorbikes taking off with ear-shattering roar. Strolled back along the Park, then up one of the side-streets. At once in suburban London. Anonymous city. Thought of fat Goldberg shuffling round the glass in the little room, rubbing his unshaven cheeks, wheezing. There he was when I entered, on the other side of the glass. I had only seen a wall there before, and now my heart leapt when I saw, through the Bride and the Bachelors, through the Milky Way and the Chariot and the Grinder and the Sieves – someone moving. (Had Moira F. not looked, not moved? Why had I not felt this when she was there? Perhaps I had

94

not wanted to feel? Had not been ready to feel?) The old dream realized. What had been in my head for so long now out there, in the world. I waited. I watched him. He came round to my side, stood beside me for a while, looking, puffing. Then he said: This is quite something. What about the right hand side? I said. That's what I want to know. But he couldn't help. Only kept repeating it was quite something, that he'd have to think about it, that it would take time to assimilate. Wouldn't be drawn. We've known each for long enough to know that silence is better if there is nothing specific to say. Please, I said to him, no hints dropped in the course of articles on other things. Let me finish in peace. We had coffee. I showed him the contents of the Green Box. Told him there would also be something specifically for him when it was done. He nodded as though he knew. We went back in and looked some more. I explained to him about the boxing-match and the waterfall and he went up close and examined the glass minutely, different areas of it, taking his time. After a while he stepped back and puffed again at my side. I think you need something on the other panel, above the oculist charts, he said at last. Or perhaps just above the arms of the scissors. What sort of thing? I asked him. He didn't know. I told him the history of the charts, my initial idea for a peephole of some sort. Maybe that's what you need now, he said, to restore the thrust of the vertical. When he'd gone, wrote Harsnet (typed Goldberg), I began to try out different possibilities. More and more convinced he's right, but not quite sure what it needs. Maybe when boxing-match problem solved this will fall into place. He urged me to come and see his new place in Brighton. Swore the sea air was doing his health good. I couldn't take London any more, he said. A sewer. An absolute sewer. You don't find it a sewer? he asked me. I don't live in London, I told him. I live in 14 Carlton Road. Besides, I told him, I like sewers. You don't have a family to think about of course, he said. I wouldn't let the children grow up in this environment. As always, he seemed to be apologizing for everything he said or did. I took a photo

95

of him through the glass. On both sides. As I looked through the viewer I had the feeling, momentarily, that it really was what I had dreamed about for so long, a sort of crystal ball in which I could call up everything I had ever known. But is that not what the mind is? A crystal ball in which one can call up the past? So is that what the big glass is perhaps? Not so much an object as a place where, the means by which, the past can be called up, the future foretold? It is for active use, wrote Harsnet, not for contemplation. That is what I was after from the start, he wrote. Having Goldberg in the room with it, as he has been in my life since that first day at college, made me grasp clearly, for the first time, just what it is I have been after, he wrote. Perhaps a perfect circle just above the oculist charts? But as if fixed to a wall there. Big glass and glossy box, he wrote. Does it need a title? Still uncertain, he wrote. Have been growing less and less interested in titles that are other than purely descriptive. Though there needs to be a little ambiguity to keep it interesting. Moira F. phoned again, he wrote. Told her definitely off for this year. Or perhaps ever. I am so disappointed, she said. So am I, I said. We both laughed. There will not be a show like it, she said. The biggest of its kind. That's life, I said. She laughed. Funny how unreal it all seems at times, he wrote. The work of the last four years. The hours in the room under the hard fluorescent light. The nightly rhythm. As if my life had stopped when the glass was started and will only start again when it is done. The plan, he wrote, and the execution of the plan. Not to be sidetracked for any reason whatsoever. Not to give in to temptation, no matter what form it takes. But difficult at times to remember why I ever made such a plan, he wrote. Or even if there was any plan at all. Or any glass at all. When I am not in the room with it, he wrote, it no longer exists. The result of others having seen it? Or what? Goldberg, pushing the typewriter away from him, wiped his face with his handkerchief and took a sip of orange juice. Then, pulling the pad towards him, he began to write. Dear Harsnet, he wrote, my son, who was only a very small boy

96

when you last saw him, happened the other day. Dear Harsnet, he wrote, my son Michael, whom you may not even remember, the fair one with the glasses. Dear Harsnet, he wrote, something happened recently which has prompted me to write to you in this unsolicited way, though God knows we were once. Dear Harsnet, he wrote, why do you persist in this rigmarole of refusing even to acknowledge my existence? What game are you playing? Dear Harsnet, he wrote, the distance between London and Brighton is not very great, and you have even been seen in the vicinity of Brighton, so why not call in on an old friend? The circle in place, wrote Harsnet (and Goldberg began to type again). Locks that part of the glass together. And finally gives charts the kind of breathing space they didn't quite have before. And gives movement to the arms of the scissors and so back through the sieves to the chariot and the moulds. Learning to work with the glass at last, he wrote (and Goldberg typed). As always happens, will have mastered it completely just when I have no more use for it. Glossy Box too vague, he wrote. Grand Verre/Boite Verte, he wrote. Sixty-four sheets of notes. Not numbered. Any order. Or reduce to 52? Keep as they are, he wrote. Do not try to tidy up. Box will contain them as glass contains what is placed upon it. More freedom with the box, but of course none of the joy of transparency. I have been walking a great deal, he wrote. Restless. Tried Danny, hoping a game would calm me down, but no reply. Glass dreadfully oppressive now. It can be made, he wrote, but it cannot be thought. The mouth is more agile than the eye, he wrote, the hand is more agile than the brain. The maximum of movement, he wrote, with the maximum of stillness. The maximum of passivity with the maximum of energy. The maximum of sameness with the maximum of difference. The maximum of silence with the maximum of noise. The maximum of significance with the maximum of insignificance. The maximum of thickness with the maximum of slimness. All painting bas relief with maximum slimness, he wrote. Wall and canvas hide that fact. Glass reveals it. Painting on wall or canvas the creation of alternative

97

worlds, he wrote. Painting on glass as delay of the world. Painting on wall or canvas as dream of plenitude, painting on glass as revelation of potential in poverty. Painting on wall or canvas as magic, painting on glass as work in the world. Work in the world as game in the world, he wrote. Game in the world as delay of the world. Delay of the world as truth of the world. Living can damage your health, he wrote. Looking at glass ditto. The glass not as addition to room, he wrote, but as subtraction from room. One hundred boxes to designated persons, he wrote, and two hundred out into the world. The important thing now, he wrote, is to finish. It has been going on for too long. Without hurry, without pause (Goethe). Do not use time as an excuse, he wrote. Do not pretend that what is laziness is really patience. Do not pretend that energy equals quality. Every genuine work an affair of the heart, he wrote. Do not prolong it beyond its allotted span, he wrote, but do not terminate it before its allotted span. The burning heart, he wrote, and the smiling face. Size clearly has something to do with its effect, he wrote, but not size as reflection of ego. Rather, size as affirmation of confidence in artistic solution. Everything visible, he wrote. No secrets. Description without place, he wrote. Stevens. Vermeer. Bonnard. If a work is bigger than a man, he wrote, it can mean either that it is trying to surpass man or that it is not afraid of being looked at. Cage in London, he wrote. Trip to Greenwich. Never separated from his plastic bag with his macrobiotic food. It changed my life, he said. I was wracked with arthritis. Had to take twenty aspirin a day for ten years the pain was so great. And within a week of switching to a macrobiotic diet the pains had eased. Now it's perfectly tolerable. Proud of his pink tie: I've worn a tie this shade for forty-five years. The Dalai Lama admired it. At the Greenwich Meridian: Every single spot on earth is the centre, that's what I've always tried to say in my music. A woman fainted when he spoke the previous day, the hall was so crowded. He told them to leave her be, she was in a better state to understand him than anyone else there. Insisted on visiting the Isle of

Dogs. Dereliction. In Egypt recently: The sand is reasserting itself. You can practically see it in the process of covering up the feeble attempts at civilization. And it's not very different in the West. Time we all moved on to Mars. We need to realize what we've done to other species. When you've botched a job a dozen times you don't hang around waiting to try one more time, you abandon it. It may be too late for man though. His father an inventor. To him a few years ago: You are my finest invention. Put him in taxi for Elizabeth Hall. Walked most of the night. His view that our character formed by our name. His cage, Bach's brook, etc. Experiment of speaking name aloud into machine and then finding face in image made by sound-waves. All the pictures he showed me looked the same messy blur but he insisted he could make out the individual features of each person. When we speak our names out loud we speak ourselves. I refused to try. Slept fitfully. Woke up struggling to say my name but somehow unable to. My tongue wouldn't get round the word or my mouth wouldn't open or something. Renewed work on splash. Sense of its triviality. Rest of glass quite dead. Sat waiting for it to come back to life. All seems so long ago and far away. Not even a question of the temptation to give up. Rather, a wonder that I was ever interested in starting. Card from Goldberg to say overwhelmed. Instead of elation felt only that it was not addressed to me. His enclosed article for Burlington on earlier work. Most significant gesture in post-war art. Legacy of Chardin. Teases us out of thought. Insignificance of Warhol and Beuys compared to. Neveu de Rameau. Nietzsche. Valéry. Jarry. Bataille. Transgression. Pornography. Rhizomes. All in four pages. Crap. Card from Moira F. enclosing dates of Festival. Sense of desolation. Walked most of the night again. Up to Hampstead and back. London compared to Paris and New York: everything shut away. Everything secret. Guilt and repression. Effort at pleasure – the Puritan absurdity. Yet my city. My feeling that no project would ever hold any interest for me again. Understood that quite clearly. As if I was holding the thought in my hands, looking at it, turning it about. Unable to get rid of the feeling that the glass belongs to another time, another person. Far away. Long ago. Goldberg with new suggestion about bottom right hand. As though now he was more concerned with the glass than I am. When I offered to let him finish it he laughed. My artist days are over, he said. He couldn't resist adding: Helped to the grave by you. It still rankles with him. But why should one incident put him off for ever? We all seek reasons. Excuses. For our lives. For how they've turned out. Perhaps the only thing I feel proud of is this: No excuses. On my tombstone: No excuses. You ruined my life (Madge). You ruined my career (Goldberg). So Harsnet. And Goldberg, pulling the pad towards him: Not all travel as light as Harsnet. Some of us have responsibilities. So Goldberg. And Harsnet: We do not 'waste time'; it is in the nature of time to be wasted. We do not take 'wrong turnings'; it is in the nature of turnings to be wrong. We do not fail, because there is no such thing as success. We are never 'not quite up to it', because there is no 'it' to be quite up to. In every case, wrote Harsnet (typed Goldberg), if we had not done what we did but something else the consequences would have been equally disastrous. In every case, he wrote, if we had done something instead of doing nothing the consequences would have been equally disastrous. In every case if we had done nothing instead of doing something the consequences would have been equally disastrous. The big glass, he wrote. Delay in glass, he wrote. Another story of disaster. Disaster to start it and disaster to go on with it. Disaster to complete it and disaster to leave it uncompleted. Disaster to be born, he wrote, and disaster to die. Wherever you turn, he wrote, there is nothing but a minefield of disasters. The boxing-match is out, he wrote. The waterfall is out. Four and a half years, he wrote. I have never spent so long on a single project. So there must have been something in it to hold my attention for so long. Perhaps there is still something in it, but not for me, he wrote. Perhaps there is still something in it, but I can no longer see it. When I think about it, he wrote, I find it difficult to remember why I ever embarked on it. When I sit in the room with it, he wrote, it's like sitting in a room with a corpse. I want it out of the house, he wrote. I realize now that that is what I want more than anything else. There comes a point in every project, he wrote, when you are tired of beating your head against the wall. There comes a time in every project, he wrote, when it becomes clear that a head is no match for a wall. Enthusiasm, he wrote, gives way to frustration, and frustration to anger, and anger to indifference. That is the time to stop, he wrote. That is the time to abandon the project. That is the time to get the thing out of the house and take up evening classes in deep-sea diving. Three steps fixed from the start, he wrote: making the glass, showing the glass, and ending it all. But now I see, he wrote (and Goldberg typed), that I must alter the emphasis of the first part. Now I see, he wrote, that I must abandon it as I have abandoned everything else. There comes a moment when you know you have done what you could do with something and everything else would be fiddling. There comes a moment when you lose interest so totally that to touch it again would be a physical impossibility. When it is too late to go on and too late to start again. From the beginning it was too late, he wrote. It was too late to begin and too late not to begin. Too late for me and too late for the world. Too late for the Bride and too late for the Bachelors. Too late for Diana and too late for Actaeon. It should have been done sooner, he wrote, but the truth is it would always have been too late. And now it is much too late to go on, he wrote, and much too late to start again. Too late for the glass, he wrote, and too late for the showing of the glass. Too late for the truth and too late to invent a lie. Too late for art and too late for the denial of art. Too late for salvation and too late for damnation. Too late for such words and much too late to suppress them. The thing about my life, he wrote, is that everything has always been too late. I was born too late and I discovered what I wanted to do too late and what I did I did too late and my death is about to come far too late. I always thought

101

it was too early, he wrote, and now I see that it is much too late. The fact that there is no right time, he wrote, the fact that it is bound always to be too early or too late, that fact is little consolation. The fact that I can write this is little consolation, he wrote. Not only is it little consolation, he wrote, it is actually a further cause for despair, for it only shows that everything is far too late, that the glass was a dream of lateness and the work on the glass was a fantasy of lateness and the belief in the glass was the madness of one who has lost all sense of the meaning of lateness. Not only did the idea come too late, he wrote, not only did the discipline come too late, not only did the resolution of individual problems come too late, but they came so late that I was not even aware of their lateness, and so they were doubly false and doubly useless and doubly meaningless. The nights in the room were false and useless and meaningless and the nights walking the city were false and useless and meaningless, the notes for the box were false and useless and meaningless and this freewheeling account of the progress of the glass is false and useless and meaningless, late and doubly late and unaware of its lateness, nothing and again nothing and worse than nothing. Letter from Goldberg, he wrote, but no point in replying. Further letter from Goldberg. Yesterday he rang the bell for a long time but no point in opening the door. Xenakis in town again but made no effort to see him. Note from Moira F. urging me to get in touch. No point in replying. As though all this had happened a long time ago. Star still twinkling but long since extinct. Goldberg at door again today. His banging roused the neighbours. Shouted that he knew I was inside. Why will you not speak to me? Why don't you open? Are you all right? Just say if you are and I'll go away. Otherwise I'll call the police. I crept to the door and, with a sudden movement, opened it wide. He stared at me in surprise. I invited him in. He seemed, for once, at a loss for words. I gave him a cup of coffee. Wouldn't answer his questions. Made no move to show him the glass. Gradually he regained his composure. Puffed at his cigarette. Invited me to Brighton. What would I do in Brighton? I said. Come and have lunch, he said. I told him I was cutting down on lunch. What's the point of having a phone if you never answer? he said. But then decided to ignore my actions, started telling me about himself, his latest article, latest book, latest catalogue introduction, latest love. He tried before leaving, as he was looking at his watch, to press me about the glass, but we know each other too well. I merely smiled and he got up, patting his face with his handkerchief, talking about the pollution of the water in London, about tests carried out and how soon everyone would have to boil drinking water first, it's turning into a third-world city, he said, a third-world country, no one will admit it but England is turning into a third-world country. I had to go to Leeds for a show just after my return from Calcutta, he said, and there really wasn't much to choose between them. Told me Moira F. had written to him, anxious for news about the glass, complaining that I never answered the phone, never replied to her letters, what should he tell her? What you like, I said. Shall I say I saw you? he asked. I told him I couldn't stop him, he was a free agent. He assured me he hadn't mentioned the glass to anyone, hadn't dropped any hints. It doesn't concern me, I told him. Feel free to say what you like. You mean the ban's off? he said. That I can talk about it? Whatever you like, I said. He was putting on his heavy overcoat, asked again casually if he could have a look at the glass. I shook my head. He left. I sent Moira a card: Glass definitively abandoned, collect as soon as possible. Two days later, card from her: Why abandoned? Please phone. Goldberg called again the day after that, charged by her to find out. What do you mean abandoned? he said. I mean I'm abandoning it, I said. Like that? he said. Unfinished? If it was finished I wouldn't say abandoned, I said. Why? he said. I've lost interest in it, I said. Interest? he said. Then: Can I see it? I took him in and watched as he studied it. You haven't taken up any of those plans about the boxing-match, he said. Or the waterfall. I stood at the window and looked down into the street. I think it's finished as it is, he said. When he had done I followed him out of the room and shut the door. He repeated he thought it was finished as it was. Said he liked all that empty space on the right. You put that peep-hole where I suggested, he said. Do you want a written acknowledgement? I asked him. No no, he said. I'm just glad I had a. Why did you abandon it? he asked again. Again I told him why. Sometimes it takes a little while to realize you really have lost interest in something, I said to him. That it isn't that you've got up on the wrong side or eaten something which didn't agree with you or just need a few days' rest. It takes a little time to see that you're not moving forward any more, either because you don't know how or because there isn't anywhere to move forward to. Of course all these things are relative, I told him, of course if you take the long perspective there's never anywhere to move forward to and all advance is illusory, but in the short perspective there comes a point when there is no option except to abandon. You feel you've failed? he asked me. He added quickly: Because I don't, you know. No, I said, I don't feel that. You've done what you wanted? he asked. I no longer know what I wanted, I said. Now it just bores me. That's why I can't go on with it. I held the door open for him. I'll tell Moira, he said. She'll be very excited. What's the point of having a phone if you never answer it? he asked me. It's awkward having to come round and not be sure of finding you. I shut the door behind him and locked it. Yesterday he came again, with her and Pearsall, the head man in Edinburgh. I sat in the kitchen and read the paper. They were in there for a long time. They came out and she gushed. Perfect. Masterpiece. And so on. Should it be called abandoned? She didn't feel, etc. Definitively abandoned, I said. Plans for Festival well under way, she said. Pride of place, etc. All that time, wrote Harsnet, Pearsall stood stiffly there without saying a word. The sooner you get it out of here the better, I said, wrote Harsnet. No problem, she said. I'll arrange for the carriers to come down as soon as I get back. Goldberg grinning. Pearsall silent. Finally they left, still not a word out of

Pearsall. Goldberg was back an hour later. They were in ecstasies, he said. It was worth waiting for all her life, she said. I didn't notice Pearsall in ecstasies, I said. It's his manner, Goldberg said. Deep down he was knocked out. Deep down he was knocked out? I said. He told you? Don't worry, he said. I could see it in his eyes. I'm not worrying, I said. They are talking about buying, he said. It's a question of raising the money. Tomorrow I go away, I said. You? he said. When did you last go away? You tell me, I said. When we went to Siena together? I shrugged. Where? he asked. Tunisia, I said. Wonderful idea, he said. Wonderful. How long for? I'll see, I said. I'll be in touch when I return. An open booking? he said. An open booking, I said. So got rid of him at last, wrote Harsnet (typed Goldberg), and went in to the glass. Now all these other eyes have looked at it I feel different about it. Now I have definitively abandoned it I begin to wonder. Sat there through the night, closing my eyes at times, then opening them slowly and allowing the glass to impose itself. Still half tempted to restart. Funny how those old temptations return. But wrong of course. Too late. Nothing more to be done. Anything else would only be a repetition. After three nights, he wrote, I again only wanted the thing out of the flat. Phoned Moira and told her I wanted it out as soon as possible; if she wouldn't have it I would find someone who would. Good news on the way, she said. Scottish National Gallery of Modern Art on point of making offer. I explained about the green box, but said nothing about this notebook. Will keep till the end. Then post to Goldberg. Or perhaps burn. Still undecided. She said she would get back to me. Possible support from Gulbenkian Foundation. Scotland would be proud to own it, she said. All I want is to get it out of the flat, I said. If you don't make up your mind soon I might just break it up. Tried locking door and ignoring it. Impossible. Of course no desire to travel. Walked a lot, he wrote, despite the cold. Snow and slush messing up the pavements. What does it <u>mean</u>, standing there in the empty room, bigger than a man? No answers to such questions. Too late to go back. Accept. First part over, second part starts. Must see it for myself in a public space. That was the plan from the start and it remains the plan. Goldberg in *Guardian* today, major new work, still to be unveiled, but those who have seen it, etc. Letter from Pizetti, what about MOMA next year, letter from Rosenblum, what about Washington after New 'York, letter from Karsten offering Hamburg. Vultures. Dear Moira, he wrote, we will have to reach an understanding. From the moment you take the big glass off my hands you will have the sole responsibility for it. Even if the Gallery does not buy it I do not wish to have anything more to do with it. After the patience of the last few years, he wrote, why this sudden impatience? As if now I know it will soon be off my hands time has started to move forward again. Cannot wait for the end. Talked to Merryman about printing sheets for green box, quite feasable as I want it, he said, samples soon. Must be linked to Edinburgh, I told him, he said no problem. Ninety-three items in box now. Good number. Dithered again about titles, use of French, etc. But all far away from me. Any decision now really quite arbitrary. Big Glass, he wrote. Gross Box. Big Glass, Glossy Box. Avoid cleverness, he wrote. Avoid wit. Avoid profundity. Call from Moira. All settled, bar details. Glass in big show of modern English art this summer, then in permanent collection of gallery. Their men to collect next week and keep in storage till show. Goldberg to write catalogue entry. He was coming to see me as I was going out. We met on the stairs. When did you get back? I told him I hadn't been away. But I thought – ? You must have misunderstood me. I wouldn't have known, he said, if Moira hadn't let fall that she'd talked to you yesterday. Seemed to feel I had personally deceived him. Asked if I intended to say a few words about the glass. I told him no. It was all in the green box. I'm not a journalist, I said. You can write what you like, I said. I told him he could use the flat till the men came from Edinburgh to collect it. I'm off, I told him. You can sit there and study it to your heart's content. It is now definitively abandoned, I said to him. But – ? he said. You know what abandoned means, I said. You've done it to women often enough. He tried to protest. I gave him the spare key. Spent the week walking along the Pembrokeshire coast. North from St David's. Midwinter. Not a soul. Gulls in plenty though. Sense of peace as I got into rhythm. No needs. No desires. Wind fierce at times. No rain. Good to be there again and for last time. On return Goldberg's note to confirm that the men had come and taken the thing away. He rang later to ask if I wanted to see what he had managed to write so far. No, I said. It's yours now, not mine. He tried to read me bits over the phone but I stopped him. Keep that for the public, I said. I wouldn't want to say anything that was wildly off the mark, he said. Anything you didn't feel yourself about it. I don't feel anything about it, I said. Note from Moira to say it had gone straight to storage in Leith. Plus date of opening. Letter later from Pearsall. We are honoured. Edinburgh is honoured. Scotland is honoured. Etc. So first part over, wrote Harsnet (typed Goldberg), and now it's a question of waiting till second is over, and so to third. *First part over, second begins*, wrote Goldberg in the margin. Never forget though, wrote Harsnet (and Goldberg typed), that we are talking here about short perspectives only. In the longer perspective, he wrote, the first part will doubtless merge into the second and the second into the third, and all three into a continuum and the continuum will turn out to be a dot. A bleep. In the longer perspective, wrote Harsnet (typed Goldberg), never forget, no beginning and no end, no Festival, no Gallery, no glass. Never forget, he wrote. But do not allow the thought to affect you either. The short perspective is where we are at, he wrote, and in the short perspective the glass is done, abandoned now but done to the best of my ability, and now the second part starts. It has to be said, he wrote, that waiting in this way is intolerable. Now the glass is gone, he wrote, the room is empty and I never go in there. Come quick, phase three, he wrote. Interminable correspondence, he wrote. Endless phone-calls from New York, Paris, Hamburg, Edinburgh, at the end of which your ear is hot and

107

red and your head splitting. To think, he wrote, that some people spend every day of their working lives talking into phones and making deals and fixing things. Or rather, he wrote, not to think about such things. Where the goal is clear one is hardly aware of the journey, he wrote. Note from Hilda: I hear you are determined to go on being outrageous. Did Goldberg tell her? Does he see her? Are you not a little old for such things? she concluded. Since she has never been outraged by anything in her life this is her way of saying that all I have left is the ability to be outrageous. How can she still not have realized that she is incapable of hurting me? The exhibition to be held in the whole gallery, he wrote. British Art since the War. Biggest ever show, glass in centre of main hall. Moira insistent that I come up and take a look. Wonderful journey from Berwick up the coast to Edinburgh. Seals basking on rocks not twenty yards from the train. Moira at station, with Bell, the Assistant Director. Very fair hair, round head, pink scalp visible, red ears. Amazing little gallery, right in the middle of the Botanical Gardens. We decided the third room would be best, Bell said, and not quite in centre, to allow viewer to get into the show before confronting it. You must realize, he said (wrote Harsnet), that we get people in here during the Festival who would not normally set foot in an art gallery to save their lives, as well as people who've travelled half way round the world to see precisely this show. All must be accomodated. I thought by the window perhaps, he said (he seemed to be able to move soundlessly over those polished floors, perhaps that is what distinguishes Assistant Directors from other human beings), but a lot will depend on what else goes into the room. Had difficulty understanding his Scots accent. We'll know better when everything is assembled here, he said. Wanted to take me out to supper but I told him I was anxious to get back. Goldberg's draft waiting for me. Usual shit. Amazed that people who get excited enough to write about art seem then to produce only banalities. But perhaps better than I imagine, the whole thing so far away from me now. Flat a little more bearable, for some reason. Perhaps the thought of the glass safely in storage in Leith and the room in the gallery waiting for it to arrive has begun to make me accept that it is no longer here, that I really have nothing more to do with it. But these are always the worst times, when you are and are not a part of it, when it is still something you feel responsible for and yet there is nothing more you can do except make sure it's shown in just the way you want. Too many disasters in the past, wrote Harsnet (typed Goldberg). But this time different because sense of show as end of second and penultimate phase. It is all going as planned then, he wrote (and Goldberg, after draining his glass of orange juice, went on typing). It is all well in hand, it is being taken good care of, but that does not stop me worrying about it all the time. Difficulty getting to sleep, he wrote, and then I wake up after barely an hour. Ironic that delay in glass should now be delay in reality, he wrote. Time flashing by like a dream since I first showed it to Goldberg, he wrote, and yet in another way so heavy on my hands. Tried to go through a few classic games but impossible to concentrate. Fixed up to have a game with Danny, then funked it. Sense in which I have to be alone. Spring, he wrote. Felt even here in Clapham. Even here the blackthorn manages to flower, the trees grow softer, rounder. Things must take their course, he wrote. I have always abided by that and I must do so now. Refused all interviews, passed them on to Goldberg, who, though apparently undergoing another marital crisis, revels in the role of spokesman for the glass. A monument to our times. Only something as big as this, something as pondered and as daring, could have freed us from the yoke of New York. Etc. Keep these notes going right through to the end, he wrote. Then mail to Goldberg and let him do what he likes with them. Proofs of material for green box in today. Very satisfactory. Publication to coincide with exhibition. Tried to read but all seems so far away from me now, as though there really was a pane of glass between me as I am now and me as I have been all my life. Dickens, he wrote. Thought this would be an opportunity to reread the whole of Dickens.

Began at the beginning, with Boz. But same effect as always: great enjoyment at moment of reading, but somehow reluctance to go on. As if once one has seen what he can do it all becomes too predictable. I sometimes think, he wrote, that the glass does not exist and never has existed. That I only dreamed it and I have not yet begun it and never will begin it. As if it was a huge joke and there was nothing except for the notes in the green box and this notebook, all referring to a work which does not exist. At the same time, he wrote, I feel that the glass, and the years of work on the glass, have separated me from my past, from the world, from all those I have known and been involved with, for better or worse, from Madge and Helen and Goldberg, from Hilda and Susan and Malone, from all those I once had something, however small, in common with, separated me totally and irrevocably, as though it was all over already and I was only a ghost, looking down on them from a great distance, knowing I would never speak to them again, and the strange thing, he wrote (and Goldberg typed), is that the two feelings can co-exist, the feeling of not yet having begun, of only dreaming of having begun, of knowing that I will never really begin, and the feeling of having finished, really finished, for the first time in my life, that these two feelings can co-exist, not one feeling for a few days and then the other feeling for a few days, but both within the same minute, almost, perhaps, together. Books that meant so much to me, wrote Harsnet, now like those books we remember from childhood, whose covers and sometimes smells can still move us, but which we find it impossible to open and read. As though almost in another language, a foreign language, Yeats and Shakespeare and even Proust, even Dante, as though there was no native language for me any more, that this is what it means to have really finished with the world, no native language spoken by you and by others unthinkingly, like breathing, and you are alone, in ways I have never been alone, you cannot summon up enthusiasm for what seems to move and torment others, however close you may have felt to them in the past, you

110

open a book and try to get involved in it and then shut it again, the language is foreign, the sentiments are foreign, it has ceased to have the power to move you, even to touch you. The glass rises between us, he wrote, it looms large in my head and everything else is on the other side of it. I see my head, he wrote, the inside of my head, as a small room in the middle of which stands the glass, dividing it in half, insulating each half from the other. I am in one half, he wrote, and the glass divides the room. What if it never existed? he wrote. What if it was never even begun? Perhaps, he wrote, it will be like that until I see it in a room which is not my own, surrounded by items which have nothing to do with me, by people I do not know. But I do not really believe that, he wrote. That is why the showing can only be the second stage, he wrote, why after the showing there will still be the third stage to come. Because it does not exist in time, he wrote, and because it was specifically designed to reveal the lack of relation between cause and effect, between one o'clock and a quarter past one, between desire and action, between a man's days and his works. Nothing happens in the glass, he wrote, and nothing can happen in the glass. One does not lead to two, A does not lead to B, there is just one and then two, just A and then B. But still time hangs heavy, he wrote. Despite the contracts to sign and the phone-calls to answer, time hangs heavy. As though, having dealt with time in the glass, all that was left to me now was the discarded skin of time. Nothing more to do, wrote Harsnet, and no time to do it in. No time to spare and yet nothing but time to be got through. Worse than an airport when the plane is delayed, he wrote, much worse than that. Nothing, he wrote. I told Goldberg I wanted to see nothing of what he had written. I wouldn't want to misrepresent you, he said, I wouldn't want to mislead the public. You cannot misrepresent me, I said to him, since you do not represent me. You cannot mislead the public, since you do not lead it. So resign yourself to saying what is, in essence, redundant and meaningless. If I didn't have alimony to pay, he said, if I didn't have the mortgage and the children, I could afford to be as high-handed as you. That's how it is, I said to him, not for the first time, wrote Harsnet, you have, you can't, so make the most of it. Told Moira I would come up for the day once she'd got it out of storage and help them decide on the best position, he wrote. Made it clear I would not be there for the opening. I said nothing about slipping in once the show was under way, that it was essential for my plans to see it with total strangers moving round it. By now she knows better than to try and persuade me. It is obvious that the end must not come during the show or even directly after it. That would look as though I wanted to boost the value of the glass by my deed. When the buzz has died down, he wrote, two months after, perhaps, November, a good month, bonfires, fog coming down, days shortening rapidly, these notes to Goldberg and then a quick finish. The beginning of a new era, Goldberg has written, and part of him really believes it, wrote Harsnet (typed Goldberg). Even someone as perceptive as he is, and there is no doubt that he is perceptive, even someone like that cannot see that it is no beginning but rather an end, cannot see that it is the end of the end, for the end began a long time ago, we have both of us lived our whole lives in its shadow, as I wrote in that little parable, *The Death of Images*, a little melodramatically perhaps, but then whatever one says will always be in excess of the facts, to say anything is already to say too much. That too I tried to say, he wrote. Green boxes like twinkling light from star long dead, he wrote. Glass itself monument to the end, the end of solemnity, the end of irony, the end of words like end, of concepts like end. 9.52 King's X, he wrote, 14.47 Edinburgh. 21.26 Edinburgh, 2.14 King's X. I notice a change, so Goldberg as we lunched yesterday, wrote Harsnet. You seem almost human these days, he said. We were eating in Bertorelli's. He wiped his plate with thick pieces of bread in the way I detest, priding himself on his psychological acumen, repeating the words change, mellowing, human. Wanted to come up to Edinburgh with me but fortunately TV appearance keeps him in London for that extra day. I'll see you there at the weekend, he said, and I didn't disabuse him. The future, he said, raising his glass, *l'chaim*. I drank to that. Back home by three thirty and at forty-three past the phone rang. Moira, in tears, hardly audible, something terrible has happened, the glass, the packers, I must get on the first plane and come and see for myself. Told her I couldn't stand planes but she insisted, I had to come as soon as possible, plane at five-twenty, she would be waiting at the airport. Rain all the way. No delays. She was there, face white and set, a young man in a white suit with her, we all got into the car in silence, she sat in the back with me, holding my hand, repeating what she had said on the phone, no idea how it could have happened, reliable carriers, often made the journey, though of course not used to handling glass of that size, that weight, they had, it seems, folded the panels over so that one lay face down on top of the other, damage not immediately apparent when they brought it up and the container was opened, only when the top panel was lifted off did they see, she couldn't go on, started to cry again in the dark beside me, lying in that state all those weeks in Leith and no one aware, just now, that day, she didn't know how it could have happened, subsided into sobs again. I put my arm round her. The young man drove in silence through the pelting rain. Then she started again about how it was the most beautiful thing, the greatest work of art she had ever been privileged to, etc., and this had happened, I had entrusted it to her and this had happened, her fault, though she had given the most precise instructions, the men were experienced, Goldberg was there at the other end, they had discussed the whole thing with him, a crew of three experienced men, thoroughly reliable, every one of them, she couldn't understand it. The young man drove impassively. The tyres swished as he took the corners. I sat and patted her shoulders, feeling like an idiot. It's only art, I told her, but she burst into tears again, said she had handed in her resignation but nothing could ever make amends, she would never be able to face herself and so on. It's only some panes of glass, I said. Shards everywhere, she said, and in the

113

bottom of the container, ground to dust, more glass, twisted wire, scrapings of paint. We got out, wrote Harsnet (typed Goldberg), and hurried through the Botanical Gardens. Inside we turned right and down into the basement. They had assembled the pieces in one of the labs. Half a dozen people standing around with funereal faces. Bell took my hand in both his and held it for a moment, exactly as though I had suffered a bereavement. Irrationally, I felt I had to cheer them up, wrote Harsnet, prove to them it wasn't as bad as all that. I didn't know how I was feeling myself, he wrote, and what any of this meant to me or would mean to me in a few hours' time. It didn't seem as bad as she had led me to expect, but it wasn't good. I asked them to leave me with it for a few hours so that I could see for myself just what the extent of the damage was. They brought me a cup of coffee. The order had clearly gone out that nothing more could be done that night, and they disbanded, some of them hugging me or pressing my hand in silent sympathy, not a scene I could ever have imagined in my wildest dreams. But Moira stayed behind. She sat and watched me, not saying anything, not even snivelling. Occasionally she would ask me if I wanted another cup of coffee. I liked the low-ceilinged room, the sense of purpose about it, everything in its place, a real room to work in. The fluorescent lighting made me feel at home. There was a noise once and I turned round. She had almost fallen off the chair in her tiredness. It was two a.m.. I went and sat down next to her and told her how I saw it. The show goes on without it, obviously, I said. That's what you will concern yourself with. Resigning is out of the question, I told her, wrote Harsnet. I'm going to need you here for a while. It'll take me a few more hours to make sure, I told her, he wrote, but I suspect the glass can be saved. Something of it can be saved. It will take time and patience, I told her, but it can probably be done. I'll tell you for sure tomorrow, I said. But she wouldn't leave. Went off and phoned her husband and came back. I took no notice of her. What had happened was obviously that the two panels had been put face to face, for some

114

unaccountable reason, with nothing in between them, and they had bounced and shattered in the course of the long journey from London to Edinburgh. But shattered in great beautiful symmetrical arcs, from the top right hand side to the bottom left of the top panel and from the top left to the bottom right of the bottom one. Ironically, the only large portion of the glass to remain intact was the blank area at the bottom right hand corner of the top panel and its mirror image at the top right hand corner of the lower panel, though in this fragment were two and three quarters of my oculist charts, the peep-hole above it, and the ends of the two arms of the scissors. Two other largeish areas were intact, of course, the top and bottom left hand corners, which included most of the Bride's head and the lower half of the glider and water-mill. The rest like some nightmarish jigsaw. Some of the bits of glass I found I was able to lay in place straight away. Others made no sense and much had gone for ever, ground into dust by the long hours of friction. Yet, by the end of the night, wrote Harsnet (typed Goldberg), a new kind of excitement. Unexpected. As though, when I had abandoned the glass, definitively abandoned it, I had secretly sensed that there would still be work to be done on it, but could not see what at the time. Moira offered to put me up but I asked her to find me a hotel nearby. As far as everyone else is concerned I'm not here and the glass is not here, I said to her. Let me work on it in peace for a few weeks and then we'll see. Strange times, he wrote (and Goldberg typed). Festival in full swing and my only concern to avoid people and get down to the lab. Not thinking of anything except the glass, he wrote. Not even trying to understand what it is I am feeling. That will come by itself. But strong sense that the shattering has changed everything. That that phone call has changed everything. Now the logic of the three stages, so carefully planned, shot to pieces. Keep Goldberg out, I said to her. That's the only way you can make amends. Keep him out, tell the press I wasn't ready to show, that's all. Just leave me alone with it and in a few weeks we'll know where we stand. But he found out, wrote Harsnet. Of course he found out. Was down there one evening when I arrived. I can't believe it, he said. I can't believe it. These are people who are supposed to know their job, he said. I should have supervised the packing, he said, but you think with professionals. That's life, I told him. Do you think you can save it? he asked, as Moira and Bell had asked. How could I explain to them that there was no 'it' to save. I was saving nothing. First there was nothing. Then there was something. Now there is something else. I'll let you know when I've had a bit more time, I said to him. On condition that you get out now and stay out. He wanted to talk but he saw I was in no mood for it. If there's anything I can do, he said. I told him what he could do was get out, and shut the door and locked it. No it, wrote Harsnet. That is what I have been coming to realize these last few days, as I have resumed my old routine of working on the glass at night and writing here in this notebook during the day. No it but something new, he wrote. Something I had not expected, never dreamed of. The lovely symmetrical arcs of breakage, he wrote, the lovely web of lines. Its beautiful unpredictability, he wrote, and its beautiful necessity. The irony of it all, he wrote. With the Milky Way I worked at chance and made chance work for me, holding up the sheets and photographing them as the air currents caught them. And the same with the shots, firing the paint-soaked matches and letting them land where they would. But it was always I who planned the working of chance. It had to be that way, he wrote, with something as big and intricate as this. Yet always the sense that because it was I who planned it it would never outgrow me. But the shattering of the glass, he wrote – I could never have done that, even if I had wanted to, the risk was too great. And yet, he wrote, now I see that it is as if the glass had been waiting for precisely this. Patience, he wrote. Don't rush. Don't stop. Work through the night, he wrote, and then write here each day, in this quiet hotel room in Great King Street, looking out across the broad street, the pavements, the railings, the elegant houses opposite. Moira then Bell offered to put me up, he wrote, promised me peace and comfort, but I told them this suited me to perfection. A small room, plenty of light, in a clean but simple hotel, ten minutes from the Museum, away from the crowds. Where better to hide? Exhibition apparently packed. Huge success. Edinburgh swarming. My joy at still having something to work at, not being a simple visitor. My joy at the thought of all those hours ahead of me in the well-lit lab. Problems everywhere but none, I think, insoluble. A matter of patience. Time. Moira has had Goldberg's catalogue photograph, taken in the flat the day before the carriers came, blown up and pinned to the wall. But I don't need to consult it, wrote Harsnet. Picking up the pieces and considering where they should go rather like mending bits of my own body. As I handle each fragment of what was once a neutral slab of transparent glass, I begin to understand, he wrote. A kind of miracle has taken place. Resurrection an embarrassing word these days but how else to describe it? Only by being shattered could the glass come alive. So that instead of standing inside my head, dividing me from the world, as it did even when I had done with it, it has finally, now it has been shattered, entered the world. It has become marked by time, he wrote. So that all my ideas about beginnings and ends have been swept away. There has been a beginning. A true beginning. Which means that there can perhaps now be a true end. Released from the prison of my will, my imagination, touched by the world, wrote Harsnet (and Goldberg went on typing), it starts to live. The final gift of grace, he wrote. Why given to me now? And how to understand it? Do not hurry, he wrote. Do not force the pace. Let it emerge, he wrote. Let its true significance emerge. Hour by hour. Day by day. Week by week. The city empty again, he wrote. No need to hide. No need to be afraid of being recognized. Autumn coming on, he wrote. Cold winds from the sea. Drizzle. By now, he wrote, according to my old plan, the old plan I thought about every day for four years, if not longer, it should all have been over: the glass, the show, the letter, the little pile of clothes. But it isn't, he wrote. And here I am, with work to do. Moira in New York with the show, he wrote. Great success there too. Those marks, he wrote. Those great symmetrical arcs and the tiny traces of webbing. Glass, he wrote, which repels life, which repels time, which is only itself, simple delay, has suddenly come alive, has taken time into itself. What happens to delay in such circumstances? he wrote. Is it simply a longer delay, as the cracks and ridges are negotiated by the eye? Perhaps a purely human delay, he wrote. You will get there in the end, you will reach the other side, only it will take time, it will take time. The sense there now, in the glass, of a natural disaster, he wrote. Withstood, but only just. How strange, he wrote, that bride and bachelors should at last have had the chance to grind away against each other through all the bumps and jolts of that long journey, when from the start my one clear rule was that they should never ever be able to establish contact. Inseparable barrier of the Cooler, he wrote. Not one but three edges between them. I suppose I thought, he wrote, that any contact would instantly destroy them both. As, indeed, in a sense, it has. I now see, he wrote, that abandoning it when I did was not a sign of failure but on the contrary, the acknowledgement that its being was to be in an unfinished state. As its being now is to be as it is, unfinished and bearing on its body the marks of its adventures. The marks of time which I could not put upon it myself. So many things to rethink, he wrote, to reformulate. So much in my life to bring into line with the new circumstances. So much that I had held to as the only possible progression to be reconsidered. Goldberg yesterday, he wrote. Coming slowly in as I was hurrying out. Sense of utter shock. The last person I expected to see here in the middle of winter. And yet somewhere inside me I had always known that he would appear for one last time. I tried to turn, get back in, but he grabbed my arm. I pushed him aside, twisted out of his grasp, and ran past him. His fat face, surprised, mouth open, as I half looked round. Then I was in the trees and running down the hill. Heard him call my name but kept going. Whole

118

thing over so quickly I wonder now if it really happened. Yet can still feel the shock of seeing him, and his grip on my coat. Now, wrote Harsnet, after three months' work I begin to understand what the shattering of the glass really means to me. How it alters all the elements of the equation. As though now, at last, it was a part of the world and I could let it go, quite simply, with no need for final gestures. The end changes the nature of the beginning, he wrote. Nothing can be explained, he wrote, it can only be told. Abandoned, he wrote. Broken. Such words take on a different meaning in relation to the glass now, as delay had earlier taken on a different meaning in relation to it. The shattering is what finally allows it to breathe, he wrote, yet it was what almost destroyed its life. The shattering a denial of the glass, of the glassiness of the glass, and at the same time an affirmation of the glass, of the glassiness of the glass. Denial because its transparency, which is its essence, is now impaired for ever. Affirmation because only glass can crack like that. Do what you can, he wrote, and then walk out of its life for ever. Looking back now, he wrote, as the year turns, I can see that the glass was always a kind of farewell, but I did not understand then what kind it was. It has taken me four years of work and all the imponderables of four years of life to find that out. One little piece at a time, he wrote, like the builders of the cathedrals, like the makers of the windows of Chartres and Canterbury. Do not hurry, he wrote, do not stop. Let life dictate. Let time dictate. Let the glass dictate. A gift, wrote Harsnet (typed Goldberg), the advent of the unexpected.